we're in here.''

Eleanor Cutler's voice sliced through the quiet house, causing Courtney to jump in surprise. She hurried on past the dining room toward the kitchen.

Pushing open the door, Courtney charged in and then came to a complete stop.

Her entire family was sitting around the kitchen table. Her mother, eyes red-rimmed and puffy, was wiping tears off her cheeks. Eric, his face even more miserable looking than usual, was patting his mother's hand. But most surprising of all was the fact that her father was there too. His thinning dark hair was mussed, his tie was askew, and he was sitting slumped over like he'd been punched in the gut.

Courtney's stomach knotted. "What's wrong?"

Jack Cutler looked at his daughter and then shook his head. Eric said nothing. It was her mother who broke the silence.

Eleanor, an attractive, petite woman in her forties, ran her hand through her brown-blond hair and took a deep breath. "You'd better sit down, Courtney. We've got some bad news. . . . ''

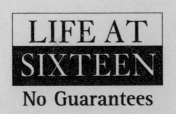

LIFE AT
SIXTEEN
No Guarantees

Books in the Life at Sixteen *Series*

BLUE MOON
SECOND BEST
NO GUARANTEES

LIFE AT SIXTEEN

No Guarantees

Cheryl Lanham

BERKLEY BOOKS, NEW YORK

If you purchased this book without a cover, you should be aware that this book is stolen property. It was reported as "unsold and destroyed" to the publisher and neither the author nor the publisher has received any payment for this "stripped book."

This book is dedicated to Kristina Domholt,
a young adult who is living proof that
the future is in very good hands.

NO GUARANTEES

A Berkley Book / published by arrangement with
the author

PRINTING HISTORY
Berkley edition / September 1997

All rights reserved.
Copyright © 1997 by Cheryl Arguile.
Excerpt from *Janine and Alex, Alex and Janine* © 1997
by Michael Levin.
This book may not be reproduced in whole or in part,
by mimeograph or any other means, without permission.
For information address: The Berkley Publishing Group,
200 Madison Avenue, New York, New York 10016,
a member of Penguin Putnam Inc.

The Putnam Berkley World Wide Web site address is
http://www.berkley.com

ISBN: 0-425-15974-4

BERKLEY®
Berkley Books are published by The Berkley Publishing Group,
200 Madison Avenue, New York, New York 10016,
a member of Penguin Putnam Inc.
BERKLEY and the "B" design
are trademarks belonging to Berkley Publishing Corporation.

PRINTED IN THE UNITED STATES OF AMERICA

10 9 8 7 6 5 4 3 2 1

CHAPTER ONE

Dear Diary,

Today is the first day of school and to be perfectly honest, I can't wait. I know this is going to be the best year of my life. It's going to be wonderful. Senior year. I'm going to make it something to remember for the rest of my life. Allison and I are trying out for the cheerleading squad today after school. I ought to have a good shot at it—I've practiced enough for it, that's for sure. I wonder if Luke will come over to watch the tryouts. I hope so. If I do say so myself, I'm pretty darned good. I mean, it would be kind of fitting for Landsdale's star football player to want to see his girlfriend make the squad. Not that I'm officially Luke's girlfriend, not yet anyway. But I'm working on that too. I've already got a bet going with Allison that Luke will take me to the Winter Ball in January. If I make the squad and I go with him, we're a sure bet to be crowned king and queen.

Courtney smiled at the words she'd written and closed her diary. She leaned over and tucked it in her bedside table. She glanced at her watch, realized that it was almost eight, and picked up her backpack. It wasn't one of those huge, ugly numbers that most of the kids had, but was small, dainty, and the perfect color blue to go with her outfit. She examined herself critically in the floor-length mirror on the back of her door. The white skirt and navy tank top with its matching cotton blouse were perfect. Not too sexy, but cute enough to show off her petite figure and good tan.

She looked around her room, her gaze flitting from the top of her oak dresser to her open closet to the bed. She hadn't forgotten anything. Courtney didn't like forgetting things. It made her feel out of control.

She hurried out of the room and down the stairs. Just as she reached the bottom, she heard a car horn. " 'Bye, Mom," she yelled in the direction of the kitchen. She didn't wait for a reply, but flew out the double front door and down the red-tiled walkway.

Allison's cute little red compact was waiting at the curb. Courtney climbed in and grinned at her best friend. "Hi. You all ready for today?"

"I don't see what you're so excited about," Allison replied. "It's only school."

"But it's going to be the best year we've ever had," Courtney exclaimed. "Besides, I don't know about you, but summer was getting pretty boring."

A tall, slender girl with white-blond hair and hazel eyes, Allison Merrill had a wardrobe that wouldn't quit. Courtney didn't think she'd ever seen her wear the same outfit twice. Today's outfit was spectacular. A pink T-shirt overlaid with a cream-colored spaghetti-strap top and a matching cream-colored short, pleated skirt showed off her long, tanned legs to perfection.

"Yeah, right. Going to the beach, shopping, and partying with our friends was really getting boring," Allison said sarcastically.

"You know what I mean," Courtney said, waving a hand for emphasis. "This is going to be a super year for both of us." She reached into her backpack for her compact.

Allison started to pull away from the curb and then stopped. "Oh, I almost forgot, my mom wanted me to find out what gardening service you use. She drove by here last week and saw your front yard. She's green with envy. Those flowers in front of your house are gorgeous."

"We use Lopez's Service," Courtney muttered, peering in her mirror. "But my mom only lets them mow the lawn; she takes care of the rest of it herself."

"She does her own gardening?" Allison said in surprise.

"Yeah, she wouldn't let Mr. Lopez near one of her flower beds for all the tea in China. Thank God she's got a hobby. If she didn't garden, she'd really be a nervous wreck." Courtney sighed silently. Her mom was really fine. Just a little high-strung and nervous. She tended to nag, too.

"Hey." Allison hit her brakes again. "There's your brother coming out of the house. Should I offer him a lift?"

Courtney glanced up from examining her face in the compact. Eric, her sixteen-year-old brother, was already heading up the street, his tall, thin, frame moving quickly, as though he too couldn't wait to get to school. Not that Eric was going to have the kind of year Courtney was going to have. He was a nerd-boy. He actually liked studying. "Don't bother," Courtney said. "He'd only sit like a lump in the backseat glaring at us. We're too intellectually shallow for the likes of my dear brother."

"He's a junior this year, right?" Allison pulled away from the curb.

"Right." Courtney thought her brother was just about the most boring subject in the world. She wondered why Allison was so interested.

"Is he still shooting for admission to Harvard?"

"So he says." Courtney shrugged. "And with his grades, he ought to have a shot at it. But even if he does get in next year, he'll still be a nerd."

"He's gotten better looking since his zits cleared up," Allison said as they drove past him. "But he's still too skinny."

Courtney was tired of talking about her dumb brother. "Just think, Allison, this time next year, we'll be in San Francisco. It'll be so exciting."

"Only if Prior accepts us," Allison cautioned. "It might be a private school, but they do have some academic standards."

"Our grades aren't that bad," Courtney shot back.

"They're not that good either. I've barely got a two point five GPA and yours isn't much better."

"Mine's two point seven," Courtney protested. "That's close to a B average. It's good enough for Prior and yours is too. At least we won't have to go to Landsdale Junior College. Even if we don't make it to Prior, we're both applying to other places and our parents can certainly afford to send us somewhere decent."

"What's wrong with Landsdale JC?" Allison said. "It's a good college. A lot of really smart kids go there. Not everyone can afford to go away to college."

"There's nothing wrong with it," Courtney said hastily. She cringed, realizing she sounded like such a snob. Darn, she was explaining it all wrong. She was just so excited about this year, so sure that this was going to be the beginning of a wonderful time in her life. "I only meant that college isn't just for getting an education. It's for having fun and expanding your horizons and all kinds of great stuff. Landsdale is okay, but we wouldn't be doing much horizon expanding right here in town."

They drove up the hill and around the high school, waving at their friends as they went past. Allison parked in the student lot. The girls hurried into the open quad in the middle of the school and joined a group of kids standing around one of the benches. They spent the ten minutes before the bell rang laughing and catching up on the latest gossip.

"There's Hillary," Allison whispered in Courtney's ear as they filed in for their first class. "She's lightened her hair. It looks good. I think she's trying out for cheerleader too."

Courtney frowned. "She'll be pretty tough competition. Hillary always plays to win."

"Are you nervous?" Allison asked.

"Sort of," she admitted as they came to the main hall. "I'll see you in the gym after school," she said as she turned to her right and Allison went in the opposite direction. "Maybe by then the butterflies in my stomach will have settled."

But the day passed so quickly for Courtney, she didn't have time to be nervous about the cheerleader tryouts. She was too busy enjoying herself. Her classes this year were going to be a breeze. She and Allison had both taken most of their really tough college prep courses in their sophomore and junior years. They'd planned it this way deliberately, so they could really enjoy their senior year.

But Courtney was disappointed when she went to the gym and saw that Luke hadn't come.

When it was her turn to do the routine she'd been practicing all summer, she pushed thoughts of Luke out of her mind and concentrated for all she was worth. She was determined to make the squad. By the level of applause after she'd finished, she was pretty sure she'd done a good job. She sat on the front bench with the other candidates, waiting for the rest of the girls to complete their routines.

"I'll post the names of this year's squad in the locker room in fifteen minutes," announced Mrs. Medrano, the p.e. teacher who ran the squad. She looked at the other three teachers on the tryout committee and smiled. "This isn't a SALT treaty we're negotiating, so it won't take too long."

"What the heck is a SALT treaty?" Allison whispered as they trudged back to the locker room to change.

"I think it's some kind of political thing," Courtney muttered. "I don't know why Mrs. Medrano always uses stuff nobody's ever heard of when she's trying to make a point."

"Some of us have heard of it," a voice from behind them said, but the tone was nice, not snippy. They turned and saw Suzanne Coontz, another senior, fall into step behind them. She laughed. "I'm sorry, but I couldn't resist having a jab at you two. How do you think you did today?"

Courtney shrugged. "I did my best. That's the most anyone can do. If I don't make it, it won't be the end of the world." But it would be; she'd die if she didn't make it.

"Me too," Allison echoed. "I'd love to be a cheerleader, but I won't slit my throat if I get edged out. You did real good, Suzanne, you've got a good shot at it too."

"Thanks." But Suzanne's bright smile seemed slightly forced. "I only tried out because Mrs. Medrano insisted. It's not really my kind of thing. Not anymore. Anyway, I'm going to hit the showers and then take off."

"Aren't you going to stay to see if you made it?" Courtney asked. Something weird was going on with Suzanne. Courtney knew for a fact that Suzanne had practiced her cheerleading routines all summer. "Mrs. Medrano said they'd be finished in fifteen minutes."

"Nah, I've got to get to work," Suzanne replied. "Good luck to both of you."

"What was that all about?" Courtney asked as soon as Suzanne had disappeared behind the metal row of lockers toward the shower.

"Haven't you heard?" Allison said as she turned to her own locker and began to dial the combination. "She can't be on the squad even if she does make it."

"Why?" Courtney sat down on the bench in front of the row of lockers and started unlacing her shoe.

"She can't afford the uniform or the camp." Allison pulled out her towel and sat down next to Courtney. "Her dad got laid off last month."

"How awful," Courtney said sympathetically. "Poor Suzanne."

"I don't know why she even bothered to try out." Hillary Steadman, who was sitting on the bench directly across from them, chimed in. "It's not like she's got a chance at all."

"Her routine was really good," Courtney said defensively.

"Yeah, but so what," Hillary sneered. "She can't even afford the uniform."

Courtney felt a wave of pity for Suzanne. Suzanne was a nice person. She'd tutored Courtney in French last year. "But isn't there some kind of fund for that?" she asked. "I mean, it doesn't seem right that just because her father got laid off she can't have a chance to be on the squad. She's practiced for months."

"Yeah, it's a tough break," Allison muttered. She pulled off her shoes and socks.

"Get real," Hillary snapped. "If you ask me, it's just one less person to compete with. Mrs. Medrano knows about Suzanne's problems. They're not going to put her on the squad."

"But isn't there some kind of benevolence fund or PTA money?" Courtney persisted. It just didn't seem fair. "There must be, otherwise Suzanne wouldn't have wasted her time trying out."

"It's not just the uniform money," Allison said quickly, "it's the fact that Suzanne has to work now. Even if there was a way to outfit her for the squad, she'd have to miss half the football games. You know how Mrs. Medrano feels about that."

"Then why in the heck did she try out?" Courtney asked plaintively.

"Because the big M made her." Hillary laughed. "She's always pushing for stuff like that. You've heard her lectures on how school activities should be for everyone, not just the rich. Seems to me, though, that if you haven't got the dough, you shouldn't waste everyone else's time."

"Speaking of money," Allison said quickly, shooting a narrow-eyed glance at Hillary, "how's the campaign for the car coming?"

Courtney frowned slightly. "Okay, I guess."

"You guess? What did your dad say?"

"He said he'd think about it," Courtney said slowly. "That usually means yes." But somehow, she had a feeling that this time there was more to it than her dad dragging his feet. She really wanted a car, but when she'd brought the subject up last night, her mother had actually snapped at her to "get off her duff and get a job." Weird, really. But Courtney was sure they'd both come around. Her mom was probably just in one of her moods. Besides, it wasn't as if the Cutler family couldn't afford it. She wasn't asking for a gold-plated yacht and a matching life jacket.

The girls quickly took their showers and got dressed. Courtney was just slipping on her sandals when she heard a commotion at the front of the locker room.

Allison stood up on the bench, craning her neck to see the front of the room over the tops of the tall metal lockers. "It's Mrs. Medrano—she's posting the list!"

They, along with everyone else, charged toward the front of the huge, cavernous room. "Let me worm my way up to the front," Allison said to Courtney. "I'm tall."

Courtney waited impatiently as Allison fought her way through the crowd of noisy teenagers. Finally, after what seemed hours, she got close enough to read the list.

Courtney twisted her hands together and closed her eyes, silently praying for it to be good news.

"We made it, we made it," Allison screamed the news at the top of her lungs.

"Are you sure my name's on it?" Courtney yelled. "Are you absolutely certain?"

"Of course I am." Allison fought her way back through the crowd. "Despite my GPA, I can read." She grabbed Courtney and hugged her. "We made it! God, I was so scared that one of us would and the other wouldn't. That would have been so awful. But we did it, we did it! All that practicing in your backyard really paid off."

Courtney's heart jackhammered against her chest. She couldn't wait to tell Luke, she couldn't wait to tell her folks. She almost wanted to make an announcement in the newspaper. She was going to be a Landsdale High School cheerleader. Her senior year and she'd finally made it!

To celebrate, they went to Harbinger's, a coffee shop/fast food joint that served as a hangout for the kids from Landsdale High. The placed was packed. Every booth was filled with kids sipping Cokes and eating burgers and fries.

"Over here," a booming masculine voice called.

They both smiled as they realized that Luke Decker and a couple of his friends were waving them to their booth.

"Wow, I wonder if he knows already," Courtney whispered.

"He couldn't. We just found out ourselves," Allison replied. "Damn, is my hair okay?" she hissed in Courtney's ear. "Jared's there too." Allison had had a crush on Jared Pronsky since ninth grade.

"You look great," Courtney assured her.

Luke, a tall, blond hunk with a set of teeth that would make an orthodonist jealous, slid over and patted the spot beside him. "Sit down," he said, looking right at Courtney. "So, how'd it go at the tryouts?"

"Great," Courtney replied, giving Allison a quick grin. "We both made it."

Luke put his arm around her and gave her a hug. "That's terrific. I'll like knowing that you're standing on the sidelines cheering me on when I make a touchdown."

"You going to be making them all by yourself?" Jared asked sarcastically. He was on the football team too.

The sarcasm went right over Luke's head. "Not completely by myself," he said seriously. "You guys will have to give some help."

Courtney and Allison giggled. Luke Decker wasn't known for his modesty. Or his brain.

Allison's smile faded as Suzanne Coontz, an apron tied around her waist, approached their booth. "You're working here?"

Suzanne nodded and whipped out her pad and pencil. "Yup, every day after school till nine and all day on Saturdays. You guys aren't the best tippers in the world, but the work is okay and it's close to school. What'll you have?"

"Just a Coke," Courtney replied.

"You work six days a week," Allison said incredulously. "But when do you get to go out and have fun?"

Suzanne smiled thinly. "These days fun to me is being able to put my feet up for fifteen minutes."

"I don't think it sounds so hard," Luke said. "I'll be practicing every day after school till after six and

I'll still have time to go out and party."

Suzanne gave him a sour look. "Yeah, I've heard about how you party."

Courtney gave Luke a quick glance to see if the barb had struck home. Luke did have a reputation for being pretty wild, at least when he wasn't in training. But Luke was grinning like Suzanne had paid him a compliment.

"When will you have time to study?" Allison persisted.

Suzanne shrugged. "Late at night, I guess, and Sundays. It won't matter if my grades slip a little. I'm going to have to go to Landsdale JC instead of UCSB. We can't afford that now."

When Suzanne left to get their Cokes, Courtney turned to Allison and said, "What was that all about? You were acting like none of our friends ever had a job before."

"I was just curious, that's all," Allison mumbled. "But you've got to admit, the only time any of our crowd ever worked was to save money for a ski trip or to help pay for a car. The gossip is that Suzanne's working to help her family keep a roof over their heads."

"My mother wants me to get a job to help buy my car," Courtney said. "But I'm hoping she was only having a bad PMS day."

"What kind of car are you thinking of getting?" Luke asked.

"Just a compact," Courtney said casually. "Something to run around in so I'm not constantly bumming rides from my friends."

"I wish I had a car," Jared said.

"What happened to the one you had?" Allison asked quickly.

"My dad sold it." Jared took a sip of his Coke. "He said the insurance on it was killing him." He grinned at Courtney. "You're not the only one who may have to get a job if they want a set of wheels. I'm going to start looking right after football season's over."

"My mom wasn't serious about my getting a job," Courtney replied quickly. She felt really bad for Suzanne Coontz, but she didn't want her friends thinking that her family couldn't afford to buy her a car. She remembered the sneer in Hillary Steadman's voice earlier in the locker room when they'd been talking about Suzanne's situation. She didn't want people laughing at her behind her back.

"My dad is," Jared said. "Damned serious."

"I wonder if Suzanne would have made the cheerleading squad if she didn't have to work," Courtney said.

"I think so," Allison said. "Lena Kay Porter made the squad and Suzanne was a lot better than her."

They stayed and chatted for a while longer, basking in the glow of congratulations from the other girls who drifted by their booth.

Just before six they left. "Are your parents going to be thrilled or what?" Allison gushed as they pulled up in front of Courtney's house.

Courtney opened the car door. "Sure they will. They want me to be happy. Besides, what a great way to end our senior year. Now all we need is for one of us to get crowned Winter Ball Queen."

Courtney waved goodbye to Allison and hurried up the walkway toward the large, two-story Spanish-style house. She opened one of the oak double doors and stepped inside. She stopped, dumped her backpack on the red-tiled entry floor, and checked her appearance in the ornate mirror over the heavy, dark, Spanish-style table her mother had found at an antique shop. Tucking a strand of blond-brown hair behind her ear, she grinned and smoothed her hands over her skirt. She wanted to look as good as she felt when she made her announcement.

The house seemed awfully quiet. Courtney turned and stared into the living room on the other side of the staircase. The fading daylight filtered in through the heavy velvet drapes, casting the room in shadows. No one sat on the elegant, moss green sofa or chairs, her mother's handbag wasn't on the glass coffee table, and there was no sign of her brother's junk littered on the thick, cream-colored carpet. Where was everyone?

She walked down the hall, stopping to peek into the family room. But it was empty too. The big-screen television was off and none of the lights on the stereo system were blinking red, so Eric hadn't been here listening to that awful reggae music on his headphones. What was going on? Her mother and her brother should have both been here. Her father normally didn't get home from work until after seven, so she hadn't expected him to be home yet. But darn it, she wanted to share her good news with someone.

"We're in here." Eleanor Cutler's voice sliced through the quiet house, causing Courtney to jump in surprise. She hurried on past the dining room toward the kitchen.

Pushing open the door, Courtney charged in and then came to a complete stop.

Her entire family was sitting around the kitchen table. Her mother, eyes red-rimmed and puffy, was wiping tears off her cheeks. Eric, his face even more miserable looking than usual, was patting his mother's hand. But most surprising of all was the fact that her father was there too. His thinning dark hair was mussed, his tie was askew, and he was sitting slumped over like he'd been punched in the gut.

Courtney's stomach knotted. "What's wrong?"

Jack Cutler looked at his daughter and then shook his head. Eric said nothing. It was her mother who broke the silence.

Eleanor, an attractive, petite woman in her forties, ran her hand through her brown-blond hair and took a deep breath. "You'd better sit down, Courtney. We've got some bad news."

Courtney wasn't sure she could get her legs to move. Was her father sick? Was he dying? Oh God, it must be cancer or a heart problem. "What is it? Is Dad sick? Are you sick?"

"No one's sick," Eleanor said firmly. "It's not as bad as that. Come and sit down."

Courtney stumbled over to the table, pulled out the chair next to her dad, and sat down. Her father's face had gone so pale that it looked like the color of charcoal after a barbecue. "Are you okay?" she asked him.

Jack gave her a strained smile. "I'm not sick, honey, if that's what you're asking. But I wouldn't say I'm okay, either."

"Honey." Eleanor cleared her throat. "Your dad and I have something to tell you."

"Oh God, you're not getting a divorce, are you?" Courtney cried. Her parents could be a real pain in the butt, but she couldn't stand the thought of them not being together. Their marriage probably wasn't perfect—her mom was kind of nervous and naggy and her dad worked a lot of hours—but surely they wouldn't split up over something that stupid.

"They're not getting divorced," Eric said impatiently. "If you'd shut up and give them a chance to talk—"

"Shut up yourself," Courtney snapped.

"Kids," Eleanor interrupted firmly, "we don't need you two fighting with each other right now. We've got enough to deal with as it is."

"What's going on?" Courtney cried. "Why is Dad home so early and why is everyone sitting around looking like someone died?"

"If you'll give me a chance, I'll tell you," Eleanor yelled. "This isn't easy, you know."

"What isn't easy?" Courtney's stomach was now doing flip-flops. Why didn't they just spit it out? If no one was sick or dying, why did they all look like they'd just buried the family dog?

"Quit interrupting," Eric demanded.

"I'm not interrupting," Courtney argued. "I'm worried. There's a difference."

"We're all worried," Jack said quietly. "And what your mother and I are trying to tell you is that things are going to change around here."

"Change?" Courtney didn't want any changes in her life. It was perfect the way it was. "What kind of changes?"

"For starters, I wouldn't count on getting that car you've been bugging them about," Eric said sarcastically. "As a matter of fact, I wouldn't count on getting as much as a pair of roller blades."

"What's he talking about?" Courtney demanded. "Why can't I have my car? I'm not asking for a Ferrari, you know. Just a cheap, basic compact so I don't have to keep asking Allison for rides all the time. I'm going to need a car this year—I've got so many activities and Allison and I aren't Siamese twins. Some of those things I'm going to be doing on my own."

Eric snorted.

Jack looked down at the table top.

"Courtney," Eleanor said impatiently, "you're not getting a car and that's that."

"But why?"

Eleanor sighed deeply. "Because your father's lost his job."

CHAPTER TWO

September 11th

Dear Diary,

There's just no other way to say it: Life sucks. Yesterday at this time, I was the happiest girl in Landsdale. Funny how things can go to hell in less than twenty-four hours. Dad lost his job. Can you believe it? Right before the start of the most important year of my life, he goes and gets himself fired. Oh heck, that sounds really selfish. I feel bad for him, honestly I do. But his getting canned sure puts a damper on my plans.

Courtney frowned at the words she'd just written and almost crossed them out. Now that she saw her thoughts written out in black and white, she felt like a jerk. She should be feeling sorry for her father, and she was. But she felt sorrier for herself. What was she going to tell her friends? She shuddered, remembering the way Hillary had sneered at Suzanne Coontz. But in all fairness, she knew most of the kids weren't as obnoxious as Hillary.

But they'd feel sorry for her. Somehow that was even worse.

She'd die before she'd have Allison or Luke or Jared talking about her in pathetic hushed whispers.

There was only one thing to do. She'd keep it a secret.

This was family business. No one need know that her father had lost his job and, no matter what it took, no one would know. Not if she could help it. She tapped her pencil against the open diary. Could she really keep it a secret? Layoffs were big deals. It might be mentioned in the local newspaper. But maybe it wouldn't.

TechniQuik, her dad's former company, wasn't in Landsdale. It was in Thousand Oaks. She didn't think any of the other kids at school had a relative who worked there. Maybe by the time anyone found out he'd been laid off, he'd have another job, her life would be back to normal, and her problems would be over.

Courtney slowly shut her diary. She'd have to lie to Allison. She cringed at the idea. She and Allison never kept things from each other. But could she trust her best friend to keep this to herself? Courtney shook her head. It was a risk she wasn't prepared to take. Allison wouldn't mean to tell anyone but sometimes that mouth of hers took off like an outboard motor and by the time Allison caught herself, anyone in earshot was drenched. No, Courtney decided not to say anything to Allison. She wouldn't tell anyone. Not till it was all over and her father had another good job.

Last night had been worse than going to the dentist and having a pop quiz on the same day. After her parents had made their announcement, they'd disappeared into their bedroom to talk privately. Eric, with a final sour look in Courtney's direction, had gone up to his room. She hadn't even had a chance to tell anyone about making the cheerleading squad.

Courtney got off her bed and dressed. She brushed her hair, finished putting on her makeup, and grabbed her backpack. Maybe she'd have a chance to tell the family the good news at breakfast.

But even though she knew her father had been laid off, it was still a shock for Courtney to walk into the kitchen and see him at the table. "Good morning," she said politely.

"Morning." Her mother looked up from her cup of coffee and gave her a wan smile.

"How's my girl?" her father said, forcing a light tone into his voice, which didn't fool Courtney for one minute.

Eric kept on eating his eggs.

"Uh, there's something I didn't get a chance to tell everyone yesterday," she began as she reached for the crystal pitcher of orange juice.

"I hope it's good news," Eleanor said, picking up her cup and taking a sip.

"Oh it is," Courtney said enthusiastically. She paused until she had everyone's full attention, and even Eric stopped stuffing food into his mouth and looked at her. "I made the cheerleading squad," she announced proudly.

Everyone stared at her blankly. Then Jack and Eleanor exchanged glances and Eric just shook his head.

"Well, isn't that good news?" Courtney prompted. "I mean, I did practice all summer. God, you're all acting like I just announced I was quitting school and running away to join a rock band." That wasn't quite true. As far as she could tell, they hadn't reacted at all. "Don't you think at least a 'congratulations, honey' is called for here?"

"Congratulations, honey," Jack said softly. Then he quickly looked down at the table.

"You don't get it, do you?" Eric said quietly.

Surprised, Courtney stared at her brother. What was he talking about? Get what? Weren't they happy for her? Even Eric, the ultimate nerd-boy, seemed to understand something here that she didn't.

"I'm sorry, honey," Eleanor said gently. "But it's out of the question now."

Courtney couldn't believe her ears. She dragged her gaze from her brother to her mother. But Eleanor's expression was dead serious. "Are you trying to tell me that I can't be on the cheerleading squad?"

"I'm afraid so," Eleanor smiled sadly. "We can't afford it. Not now."

"For goodness' sake," Courtney sputtered. "Dad only got laid off yesterday. Surely we're not so desperate that you can't afford a few hundred bucks for a uniform."

"Of course we can, honey," Jack said soothingly. "I'll get another job and I'm going to call the personnel department at work today and see about borrowing against my pension."

"You'll do no such thing," Eleanor snapped at her husband. "Especially not for something as stupid as a cheerleader's uniform."

"But, honey," Jack argued, "we already agreed that we'd have to borrow to make the next mortgage payment. Surely we can squeeze a little out for Courtney's uniform."

Courtney was stunned. Were her parents saying they had no money? No money at all?

"I'm not saying we shouldn't borrow against the pension," Eleanor said, "especially as we've no idea how long it's going to take you to find another job. That pension money may have to last us a long time. We're not blowing what little we've got on a uniform so Courtney can prance around in front of a bunch of football players and leering high school boys."

"But I worked hard to make the squad," Courtney cried.

"I know you're upset, Eleanor," Jack said firmly, "but Courtney's right. She did work hard. It's not her fault I got laid off."

"That's an asinine thing to do to please a teenager," Eleanor replied. "Especially as it isn't just the cost of the uniform we're talking about. There's the cheerleading camp the first weekend in October. With the plane fare and the hotel and the workshops, that'll cost over five hundred dollars."

Jack held up his hand. "Let's see if I can borrow against the pension first," he said, "then we can start worrying about what we can and can't afford for our children."

Courtney should have felt elated. She'd won this round and she knew it. But she felt lousy. "Dad," she asked softly, "uh, if you don't mind my asking, why did you get fired?"

"It wasn't your dad's fault," Eleanor said quickly. "His whole division is being shut down."

"They're closing my operation and moving the technical jobs to India," Jack explained.

"India?" Courtney said. "But why?"

"So they can make big bucks," Eric interjected. "Labor costs are cheaper there, so corporations fire their employees here and move business overseas. It sucks. Someone ought to do something about it. Thousands of American jobs have been lost like that."

Courtney looked at her father. "Is this true? You're losing your job so that TechniQuik can make more money? But you've worked so hard for them . . . put in thousands of hours . . . how can they do that? You've been there over twenty years. That's not fair. One of the reasons that company is profitable is because people like you have worked their butts off."

Jack shrugged. "I know, honey, but that's the way it is. Life isn't fair sometimes."

"You'll get another job, won't you?" Courtney asked worriedly.

"Sure I will," he replied heartily. "I've got plenty of friends in the computer industry. Today I'm going to put some feelers out and see what's available."

School was a nightmare. Courtney forced herself to smile and laugh and pretend that everything was just hunky-dory. But by the time she'd finished her last class and was heading over to the gym to find Mrs. Medrano, her cheeks hurt and she had a pounding headache.

She was sure she'd kept her secret well hidden, though, since even Allison hadn't noticed there was something wrong. Before leaving for school this morning, she'd cornered Eric and made him promise to keep his mouth shut about their circumstances. Eric's reaction hadn't been what she'd expected. Instead of being embarrassed about their father losing his job, Eric had been pissed. Angrier than she'd ever seen him. He'd actually thought they ought to tell everyone!

"Why should we be uptight about it?" he'd snapped. "People ought to know what TechniQuik and other corporations are doing to workers in this country. Maybe if enough people know about it, they'll do something." Courtney had had to do a lot of fast talking to get him to agree to keep his mouth shut.

She pulled open the outer door of the gym and walked through the foyer, past the trophies for the girls' volleyball team gleaming in their glass case, and down the hall to the offices. Mrs. Medrano's door was closed. Courtney knocked.

"Come in."

She stepped inside. Mrs. Medrano, her glasses perched on the end of her nose and her dark hair spilling out of its clip at the nape of her neck, looked up and grinned. "Hi, Courtney. Did you need to see me about something?"

One thing Courtney liked about the teacher, other than the fact that she was nice and friendly, was that she always got straight to the point. "I'd like to talk to you. If this isn't a good time, I can come back tomorrow." She crossed her fingers for luck. She didn't want to come back; she wanted to get this over with.

Mrs. Medrano's eyebrows rose. "Have a seat. I'm busy but not swamped. This is as good a time as any." She paused while Courtney sat down opposite her and then said, "What's up?"

"Well," Courtney said slowly, "I've got a problem with the cheerleading squad. I mean, it's not a problem that's serious or anything, but I wondered if maybe there was some way . . . some way I could be on the squad without being on the squad right now."

Puzzled, Mrs. Medrano took her glasses off and laid them on the desk. "I don't understand."

Courtney cleared her throat. She had to be careful here. She didn't want to lose her spot on the squad, not if her father really could borrow against his retirement. "My parents want me to concentrate on academics this year," she began, "but I'm softening them up, you see. So I was wondering if I could let you know tomorrow or Monday if they're going to let me be on the squad."

Mrs. Medrano didn't say anything for a moment. "Courtney, didn't your folks know you were trying out? They signed the permission slips."

"Of course they knew," Courtney replied quickly. The last thing she wanted was the teacher calling her mother and asking if the signature on the slip was genuine. "But then they kind of had a change of heart. For some weird reason, my mom seems to think that cheerleading might take too much time away from my studies. But I've just about convinced her she's wrong. She'll come around. I mean, it's my senior year and she knows this is important to me. I've almost got her talked into letting me be on the squad. All I need is another day or two."

"I see," Mrs. Medrano said softly. "Well, if you're not going to be on the squad, I really do need to know so that I can contact the alternate. Whoever is on the team is going to need time to get fitted for a uniform and make camp reservations and all that kind of thing."

Courtney's face fell. She'd been afraid of this. Because Landsdale High was one of the few schools in the area that picked its cheerleading squad at the beginning of the academic year, not at the end of the previous year, timing was always tight. *Darn.*

"I think I can wait a day or two," Mrs. Medrano continued. "But I'll have to know for sure by Monday morning, is that clear?"

"Thank you, Mrs. Medrano," Courtney gushed in relief. "This is very important to me. I really appreciate your giving me a chance."

Mrs. Medrano smiled kindly. "Do you mind if I ask you something?"

"No, go right ahead."

"Now, don't be embarrassed, but if your mother's reservations about your being on the squad is based on the cost of the uniform or the camp . . ."

Blood rushed to Courtney's head. Oh God, she knew. Eric, that little snitch, hadn't kept his mouth shut and the word must be all over school. She was going to die, simply die of humiliation.

". . . then we have a benevolent fund you can draw upon," Mrs. Medrano continued. "It would cover the cost of everything."

"That's not the problem," Courtney blurted out. "Really it isn't."

"Courtney," Mrs. Medrano said lightly, "I'm not saying it is. But there are a lot of kids whose parents have been laid off and who can't afford the extracurricular activities. It's nothing to be ashamed of—"

"But that's not my situation," Courtney interrupted. There was just a chance that Eric hadn't mouthed off. This was beginning to sound like a standard teacher's spiel. "My situation's entirely different. But thanks for the offer." She stood up quickly. She had to get out of there. She didn't like the way the woman was staring at her. "I'll let you know by Monday for sure."

"Fine. I'll be here before school—you can either call or drop by."

Courtney fled. She stumbled out of the building as fast as she dared. She could feel the heat in her cheeks, feel the sick crawl of humiliation ooze into her stomach. If Eric had told anyone, she'd kill him.

She hurried down the concrete walkway and around the corner. Her brother Eric was sitting on a bench in front of the building, waiting for her. He got up when he saw her. "I thought we could go home together," he said. "Allison's already left, so we'll have to walk."

She stared at him in surprise. Eric hadn't waited to walk home with her since they were in grade school. "Okay. Did you tell anyone?"

He knew what she meant. He shook his head as they started across the quad. "I said I wouldn't and I didn't. How'd it go with the pep coach?"

"Are you sure? Not even Buddy?" she persisted. Buddy Brock was Eric's best friend and an even bigger nerd than her brother. But he was a nice kid, even if he did have zits bigger than marbles.

"I didn't say anything to anyone," Eric insisted. "I think it's stupid to try and hide it though. Dad didn't do anything wrong. Seems to me we ought to be telling anyone who stands still for thirty seconds how American workers are getting screwed by corporate greed. But I did what you asked. I haven't told anyone and I'm not going to."

Courtney didn't understand Eric when he talked like that. But they were very different people. She was sociable and popular; he was studious and nerdy and didn't give a hoot what people thought. "Thanks. It is important to me." She slanted him a puzzled glance. "What did you mean about workers getting screwed by corporate greed? Is that what's happening to Dad?"

"You bet," Eric replied. He shifted his backpack as they made their way down the steps and out onto the sidewalk. "He's not the only one. It's happening everywhere. Don't you ever watch the news or read the papers?"

Courtney ignored that question. There was only one thing she wanted to know. "But Dad will get another job?"

Eric stopped abruptly and so did she. He stared at her for a moment. "Sure," he finally said, "he'll find another job. But maybe it won't be as good as the one he lost. He might make a lot less money. That's par for the course these days."

"Allison called," Eleanor said to Courtney as she and Eric came into the family room. "She wants you to call her back."

Eric headed for the kitchen. Courtney dumped her backpack on the couch and headed for the stairs, planning on making her call from the privacy of her room. But she hadn't gone more than a few steps when her mother's voice stopped her.

"Call Allison back later," Eleanor said. "Your dad and I want to talk to both of you."

Eric, looking apprehensive, swung back from the hall. He glanced at Courtney and shrugged. "Another family powwow, I guess," he muttered.

"Where is Dad?" Courtney asked.

"He'll be right here," Eleanor replied. "He's upstairs making a phone call. You guys just sit down on the couch."

"Can't I get something to eat while we're waiting?" Eric complained. "I'm starving."

"You're always starving." Eleanor smiled. "Besides, here comes Dad now."

Jack Cutler came into the room. "Good, you're home." He waited for Eleanor to sit down in the overstuffed easy chair and then plopped himself down on one end of the couch. They formed a half circle around the coffee table.

Courtney didn't like this. More bad news? But what more could there be? They were already up the creek without a paddle.

"Your mother and I," he began seriously, "debated about whether or not to tell you this, but as you're both almost adults, we decided that hiding the truth from you would be wrong."

"Hiding the truth about what?" Eric asked cautiously.

"About our financial situation."

"But we know you've lost your job," Courtney said. "So what else is there to tell?"

Jack smiled wearily. "Plenty. The fact is," he glanced at his wife, who nodded as though to give him moral support, "we're flat broke."

"Flat broke?" Courtney echoed in confusion. "What does that mean? Don't you get severance pay or something? Don't we have a savings account or an IRA or investments—"

"We don't have any of those things," Jack admitted. "We used up our savings redoing the house last year, I cashed in my IRA to buy Mom's car, and the company isn't legally obligated to give out severance pay. They didn't. They just fired us all."

Courtney hadn't thought anything could shock her as much as last night's news, but she'd been wrong. She went utterly still, terrified that if she so much as moved, she'd shatter into little pieces.

"Can we make this month's bills?" Eric asked worriedly.

"Some of them," Jack said. "I do have some vacation pay coming. But we won't be able to handle the mortgage or the second."

"Second?" Courtney repeated. "What's a second?"

"It's a loan against equity," Eric said quickly. "Mom and Dad took one out five years ago. Lots of people have seconds. You get one based on the idea that your house will increase in value. But instead of the value of our house going up, it went down, along with everyone else's house in California."

"I'm sorry, kids," Jack said. He shook his head. "I know this is pretty tough for you to handle. . . ."

"But you'll find another job, won't you?" Courtney asked desperately. She wasn't worried now about making the cheerleading squad—she was worried about having to sleep in the family car.

"I hope so, honey," her father replied glumly. "But I called my contacts and it doesn't look good. One of them is unemployed himself and the second guy, Arthur Morrison, is worried that they're going to close his office."

"But you've got a college education and twenty years' computer experience," Courtney persisted. "Surely that counts."

"Not these days," her mother said softly.

"But what happened to all our money?" Courtney felt tears well up in her eyes, so she blinked hard to keep them from falling. "We've always had money. Why don't we have a savings account and investments and—and—"

"Stop it, Courtney," Eleanor said sharply. "You're making your father feel worse."

"It's okay, honey," Jack said to Eleanor, reaching over to pat her hand. "Courtney has a right to be upset. She's scared. We're all scared." He smiled at his daughter. "We used to have all those things, but like I said, we redid the house last year and that used our savings. I sold off my investments bit by bit over the past few years to keep us in the lifestyle we've become accustomed to." He shrugged. "Financially, things have been tough for the past few years. I haven't had a raise, the cost of everything from food to shaving cream has gone up, and we dipped into our nest egg just to make ends meet. I didn't expect to lose my job."

"Where do you think that big clothing allowance you got every month came from?" Eric put in. "And the money for all those weekend ski trips and getting your hair and nails done—"

"I wasn't the only one spending around here," Courtney said defensively. "What about your computer and all those video games and CD-ROMs—"

"Stop it, both of you," Eleanor commanded. "All of us spent money. It takes a mint to keep this household running and your dad did a good job of taking care of us all these years. But we're not here to worry about the past, we're here to plan what we have to do to survive."

"If we do survive," Jack muttered.

"Knock it off, Jack," Eleanor said firmly. "Of course we'll survive. Survive and prosper. Maybe we won't live the way we used to, but that doesn't mean that we can't enjoy life. Now stop pulling all those long faces. We'll get by. We're four capable, intelligent adults and I refuse to believe we're going to end up sleeping in our car or lining up at the soup kitchen."

Surprised, Courtney looked at her mother. Yesterday she'd have bet a month's clothing allowance that this kind of thing would have had Eleanor Cutler prostrate with nerves. But instead her mom was acting like a commanding general. Weird. Really weird. "All right," Courtney said. "What do we have to do?"

"The only thing we can do." Eleanor grinned at her. "Pull in our belts, pinch every penny till the buffalo screams, and try to find jobs."

Courtney avoided calling Allison back. She was too depressed. Tonight she didn't think she had it in her to hide it. She sat on the foot of her bed, staring at herself in the mirror. There was a soft knock on her bedroom door. "Come in."

Eric came in and closed the door quietly behind him. "Hey," he said. "How are you doing?"

"Lousy. You?"

"The same." But he grinned.

"Can I sit down?" He looked at the chair in front of her dressing table. "I want to talk about our situation."

"Feel free," she nodded. "But what else is there to say? We're broke, we might lose our house, and we're not supposed to worry because we're four reasonable adults."

Eric sighed and brushed a lock of hair off his forehead. Courtney noticed again that his acne had cleared up. He was still tall and gangly, but at least his face didn't resemble a gravel road.

"I think I know where you can find a job," he blurted. He shifted, uncomfortable on the padded satin seat. "There's a Help Wanted sign in the window at the Victorian Café. It's been there for a couple of days so I don't think they're having much luck finding a waitress."

"A waitress?" She gaped at him. "But I don't know how to wait tables. Why would they hire me?"

"It couldn't be too hard to learn," he pointed out. "Josh Bennett's sister is a waitress at Morgan's in the mall, and she's practically retarded."

"Gee thanks," Courtney said sarcastically. The thought of waitressing made her sick. She flashed back to Suzanne Coontz and shuddered. But at least the Victorian Café was off the beaten track. It was over on the other side of town. "Do you think I'd have a shot at it?"

"Sure, why not? I'm going over there tomorrow to put in an application at Bongo Bongo Pizza. That's just across the street from the Victorian."

Courtney thought about it. She didn't really have much choice. If she wanted any fun at all her senior year, she was going to have to pay for it herself. She thought of not being able to afford a yearbook or a senior class ring or to go to the Winter Ball, and she made up her mind. She'd apply for that job. The worst that could happen was that she wouldn't get it. Then she thought of another problem. "But saying I got the job, or you got a job at Bongo Bongo, how would we get back and forth to work? Dad lost his company car. Between him and Mom, we'll never get a chance to use the van."

"Easy," Eric said confidently. "We take the bus to work."

"The bus?" Courtney bit her lip. "But isn't that

dangerous? I mean, we'd have to work some night shifts. . . ."

"No problem. They always ask you what shifts you can work when you apply for a job at these kinds of places. Here's what we'll do. We'll both put down that we can work the same nights and the same hours. That way, we'll be able to ride home together. Even if we had to work late, with two of us, taking the bus should be okay. I mean, how many serial killers go after two people at once?"

CHAPTER THREE

September 12th

Dear Diary,

Can you believe it? I'm going to spend the first Friday night of the school year applying for a job. That's right, I'm not going to the Senior Welcome Dance, I'm not going out with Allison or Luke, I'm going to the Victorian Café. This is the pits! But the bottom line is, if I want any money at all this year, I'm going to have to earn it myself. I've come up with a good story to tell Allison and the rest of the kids. I'm just hoping they'll believe me.

Courtney sighed, put her diary away, and picked up her backpack. She might as well get moving—Allison would be pulling up out front any second. On her way downstairs, she passed her mother coming out of her room. Her eyes widened in surprise. Eleanor was dressed in a beige suit, a brown blouse, and matching pumps. "What are you all dressed up for?"

"I've got a hot lead on a job at a nursery over on

Elm Avenue," Eleanor said excitedly. "I want to be waiting at the front door when they open up. The early bird gets the worm, you know."

"A nursery? You mean like a preschool?" Courtney leaned against the top railing of the stairs.

Eleanor laughed. "No, silly. I mean like a place where they sell plants. You know how I love to garden," she said as she brushed past her daughter and continued down the stairs. "I might as well try and find work doing something I know about, and believe me, I do know plants."

"But Dad's only been unemployed for two days," Courtney said. "What's the rush? Maybe he'll find something soon."

Eleanor stopped in the middle of the stairs and turned to look at her daughter. "Maybe he will, but I'm not counting on it. Jobs like the one your dad had don't grow on trees. There are dozens of people just as qualified as he is out there looking. The odds of him finding something with a comparable salary right away are pretty slim." She turned and continued down to the entry hall.

Courtney was right on her heels. *A nursery*. People would see her mother working there. People she knew. Maybe not her friends—plant shopping wasn't something they did all that often—but their parents were bound to see Eleanor Cutler at a place like that. She did some quick thinking. Maybe this could work out. . . . Maybe her mom getting a job working with plants would reinforce the story she was going to be handing out to her friends.

"Do I look okay?" Eleanor asked anxiously as she dashed over to the mirror in the foyer to check her appearance. "I really want this job."

"You look great, Mom," Courtney said sincerely.

She went past her mother and grabbed the door-knob. "I really hope you get it too," she added, pulling the door open and stepping outside. "You'd be great at it. See you tonight."

Her timing was perfect. Allison pulled up just as she got outside. Courtney hurried to the car, tossed her backpack in the backseat, and climbed in. "Hi."

"Hi," Allison said. "How come you didn't call me back last night?"

This was just the opening Courtney was looking for. "I couldn't," she replied. "I was too upset."

"Why? What happened?"

Courtney sighed dramatically. "My parents and I were talking."

"About the car?" Allison asked. She flipped her turn indicator on and pulled into the left lane.

"No, about how immature I am," Courtney said evenly. She'd thought she might try to make her voice shake at this point in the conversation, but as Allison was concentrating on getting them to Landsdale High in one piece, Courtney didn't think her efforts to be maudlin and miserable would be properly appreciated.

"Oh," Allison laughed. "One of those kinds of talks. Big deal, I have those with my folks all the time."

"But this is serious, Allison," Courtney said earnestly. "My parents have flipped. Dad's gone into some kind of midlife crisis, Mom's decided to try and get a job at a nursery, and they've taken it into their heads that me getting a job would be good for my character."

"Are you kidding?" Allison yelped, flashing Courtney a quick incredulous glance before jerking her gaze back to the road. "You're not serious, are you?"

"Deadly serious," Courtney replied. "My dad's thinking of quitting his job, Mom's going to work, and I've got to quit the cheerleading squad and find a job myself."

"Jeez," Allison cried. "They have gone off the deep end. What are you going to do?"

"I don't have any choice," Courtney replied. "If I want them to pay for me to go to Prior College next year, I've got to do what they ask." A wave of guilt washed over her as she realized she was making her folks sound like selfish monsters. But darn it, what choice did she have? She wasn't going to let her friends know the truth, that they were flat broke and her dad had been fired. It was much better to let everyone think her parents were going through a middle-aged crisis of some kind. Courtney crossed her fingers and watched Allison's face.

"But why do you have to quit the cheerleading squad?" Allison wailed. "If you're not on it, we'll get stuck with Hillary Steadman. She's the first alternate."

"I know, but there's nothing I can do about it. My parents are serious. They want me to concentrate on academics and get a job. That's all there is to it."

"Darn it," Allison snapped. "That's not fair."

Courtney shrugged and relaxed back in the seat. Allison believed her, she could tell. Oddly enough, the thought of not being on the squad didn't bother her as much as it had at first. But she still felt funny. As Allison pulled the car into the student parking lot, Courtney realized the queasy feeling in her stomach was guilt. Or maybe shame. Telling lies wasn't as easy as it sounded.

Living a lie might even be worse.

• • •

"You ready?" Eric asked Courtney when they met on the school steps after school. "There's a bus coming in ten minutes. If we hurry, we might just about make it."

Courtney glanced around, wanting to make sure none of her friends were hanging around. Today had been pretty lousy. First that ugly lie to Allison, then having to face Mrs. Medrano and tell her she definitely wasn't going to be on the squad, and now sneaking around to make sure none of her friends saw her getting on a bus. Peachy, just peachy. "Yeah, I'm as ready as I'll ever be. Uh, where do we catch it?"

"Down in front of the library," Eric explained, shifting his backpack and starting down the stairs. "It's not that long a ride. Did you write down the hours like I told you?"

"Yeah. How many hours did you put down?" She followed him toward the street.

"What we agreed on, twenty." Eric stuck his arm in front of her as they got to the corner, keeping her from going into the crosswalk. "Watch it, Talbot's coming around the corner in that souped-up muscle car of his." He glared at the bright red Camaro as it whizzed past. "Jeez, that guy's a jerk. His I.Q. is smaller than his gas mileage. He's going to kill someone one of these days."

Courtney was a little surprised by her brother's gesture. "Uh, thanks," she mumbled as they continued across the street. "I put down twenty hours too. The same ones you did."

"Did you include Friday and Saturday nights?" Eric asked suspiciously.

"Yes," she snapped. "But I don't see why we have

to put both nights down. For crying out loud, when am I going to get to go out with my friends?"

"That's the whole point, C.C.," Eric said quickly, using a pet name he hadn't called her in years. "No one wants to work those nights. So if we're willing, we've got a chance at the job. Do you remember everything else I told you?"

Courtney would have liked to tell her brother to bug off, she wasn't a child and she didn't need him to tell her what to do. But the truth was, she did need him. Eric read books and magazines constantly. No doubt he'd spent the past couple of days researching the best way to find a job if you were a teenager and totally inexperienced. "I remember," she replied. "I wore this lame outfit to school today, didn't I?" She glanced down at the simple, navy blue A-line skirt and the white blouse and sighed. Eric had told her the importance of looking professional at job interviews. This outfit was boring but serious. "And I'll be sure to act enthusiastic, tell them I can clean grill pans with my bare hands, carry seventeen steaming hot plates, and never lose my temper when some traveling salesman tries to pinch my ass. Will that do?"

"You don't have to be sarcastic," Eric muttered as they walked up to the bus bench. "I'm only trying to help."

"I'm sorry," she said dumping her stuff on the bench. "It's just that I really hate having to do this. You've been really cool about the whole thing. Now let's just hope we land these jobs. Otherwise this school year will go right in the toilet."

The Victorian Café and Bongo Bongo Pizza were on opposite sides of a busy intersection. It wasn't the worst section of town, but it wasn't the best either.

"Good, the Help Wanted sign is still there," Eric said. He grinned at his sister. "I'll meet you here when you're through."

"Why don't you just come into the café?" she asked, suddenly feeling butterflies the size of elephants in her stomach.

"Because having someone my age show up either before, during, or after your interview would damage your chances of getting the job," Eric replied. "You have to go to job interviews on your own; it's what all the articles I read recommended. Don't look so stressed—you'll do just great."

She nodded and watched him jog off across the street. Taking a deep breath, she walked over to the glass door of the coffee shop and pushed it open. She wrinkled her nose slightly as she stepped inside. The air was heavy with the scent of frying oil, hamburger, and onions. The place might be named The Victorian Café but it smelled more like a greasy spoon.

Directly opposite the front door was a long counter with stools. A cash register sat on one end. Across from the counter, a row of bright red booths ran the length of the room, offering patrons a stunning view of Twin Oaks Boulevard. To the left of the register and running along the opposite wall was another row of booths. Several tables covered in red-and-white-checked tablecloths filled the floor space between the booths and the counter.

A tall, blond girl who looked to be about her own age was swiping the counter with a wet cloth. Courtney plastered a smile on her face and walked toward her. "Hi," she said brightly.

"Hi," the girl said. "Can I help you?"

"I'd like to fill out an application for the waitress job," she said firmly.

"Sure, have a seat at the counter and I'll go get one." She started toward a swinging door located a few feet behind the register and then paused. "You ever waited tables before?"

Courtney shook her head. "No."

"Damn," the girl muttered. "I was hoping you had some experience."

With that she disappeared. A few moments later she was back. She plopped the application down in front of Courtney. "You ever worked before?"

"Babysitting," Courtney mumbled.

"Heck." The girl frowned. "That don't count. But go ahead and fill out the application anyway. At least you didn't show up with a bunch of bikers and I don't see any tattoos. Fill it out and I'll let David— that's the night manager—know that you're here. He'll probably want to see you."

Courtney grimaced when she finished filling out the application. It looked pathetically empty. All the spaces under "work experience" and "refer- ences" were empty.

She waited for what seemed hours, but was in actuality only a few minutes, before the door from the kitchen swung open and a good-looking hunk who couldn't have been much older than her came walking through.

The hunk was tall, dark-haired, and had a lean, intelligent face. The waitress flagged him down and pointed to Courtney at the far end of the counter.

"Hi. I'm David Nicks, the night manager." He ex- tended his hand but didn't smile. "Lannie tells me you've filled out an application for the job opening we have."

Courtney held her own smile in check as she shook hands with him. Maybe smiling was a no-no during interviews. "Yes, it's right here," she handed him her application.

"Do you have time to be interviewed now?" he asked.

"Sure, that's why I waited."

"Good." He scanned the page, his face creasing slightly in a frown. "You're a high school student?"

"I'm a senior."

"Do you have a work permit?"

"I can get one," she replied.

"Ever worked before?" he asked.

"Only babysitting," she said. Technically, she'd never even done that, but she and Eric had discussed the topic and even he'd agreed that as it wasn't the sort of thing a prospective employer could check easily, it was best to say she'd done it.

He raised his eyebrows. Courtney had the distinct feeling that he didn't believe her.

"But I'm willing to work hard and learn," Courtney said quickly, afraid he was going to dismiss her out of hand. "And I'm willing to work any hours you need—"

"What hours could you work?" he interrupted.

"Every day after school and on weekends," she replied firmly. That was more than she and Eric had agreed to, but darn it, she wanted this job. She didn't know why, but she did.

"Do you have any references?" he asked.

"I've never worked before—" she began, but he cut her off.

"I mean character references," he explained. "You know, people who will vouch for you personally. Neighbors or teachers, people like that. We need someone who's responsible, who'll show up for their shifts and not call in at the drop of a hat because one of their friends has invited them to a party."

"Sure," she said quickly, though she had the impression she was wasting her time and he'd already decided not to hire her. "I've got those. I didn't realize that's what the reference section on the application meant; I thought it meant work references."

"It's okay," he said easily, giving her a quick grin, "that's what it does mean." He handed her the application back. "Give me a couple of names. I'll be back in a minute; I've got to check something in the kitchen."

Courtney stared at the blank space and wondered why she was bothering. He wasn't going to hire her. She could see it in his eyes. He wasn't the least impressed with her pathetic qualifications, and for once her looks hadn't earned her any points. This guy might be a hunk, but he was deadly serious. She wondered if he was as young as he looked. She'd have pegged him at eighteen or nineteen, but he couldn't be that young and be the night manager.

She pulled the pen back out of her purse and hesitated. What names could she give? She didn't want any prospective employers calling her friends—they'd think it was a big joke. She thought for a minute, mentally going through a list of possible candidates. Finally, she put down her next-door neighbor, Mrs. Persy, and Eliza Lindstrom, the librarian at her local branch. Both of them had known her for a long time. They'd have to do.

David came back just as she finished. She handed him the completed application and he glanced at the references. "Okay," he said, "I'll be in touch.

There's still a couple more people I have to interview, but I'll let you know."

"Thank you," she said solemnly. "I'd appreciate that. Uh, when do you think you'll make a decision?" Her brother had told her to get that information if she could.

He shrugged. "As soon as I can. Don't worry, I'll let you know, one way or the other."

"David," the blond waitress called, "there's a delivery in the back you've got to sign for."

Without a word, he turned and hurried to the back of the restaurant. Courtney picked up her things and trudged out.

Eric was waiting for her at the corner. A huge grin split his face and he was practically humming with excitement. "I got it!" he cried. "They hired me on the spot. I start tomorrow night, can you believe it?"

She was genuinely pleased for her brother. "That's great." They started walking toward the bus bench a few yards up the street. "I wasn't quite as lucky."

"What happened?"

"Nothing, really. I filled in an application, had an interview, and failed to impress him with either my eagerness or my personality."

"Did he say you didn't have the job?" Eric asked.

"No, he said he'd be in touch," Courtney admitted. "But I could tell that he didn't want to hire me. He's got other interviews set up. Let's face it, without work experience, I don't stand a chance."

Courtney couldn't get David Nicks out of her mind. She'd thought about him all weekend. She'd spent most of the time alone. Allison and the rest of her friends were all busy with cheerleading or football practice and she hadn't felt like going out on her own. So she'd stayed home and watched old movies from her dad's extensive video collection. It hadn't been a good weekend, but all things considered, it hadn't been that bad either.

She was still thinking about David when she came home from school on Monday afternoon. It wasn't just his looks that had her daydreaming through English class. There was something about him . . . maybe it was the force of his personality or that at his age he was already out in the world and operating as an adult. She shook her head as she opened the door and stepped inside. She might as well push him out of her mind; she wasn't likely to see him again. "Hey, I'm home," she called. "Is anyone here?"

"In here." Her mother's voice came from the kitchen. "How was school?"

"Fine." Courtney headed for the refrigerator. "How was your day?"

"Great!" Eleanor beamed. "The nursery called— I got the job! Isn't that fabulous? I start tomorrow."

"Congratulations," she said sincerely, taking a can of root beer and closing the door. "You and Eric have really lucked out. Now, if Dad and I can just find something . . ."

"Your dad's at an interview right now," Eleanor told her.

Courtney perked up. "He's got a job interview? That's wonderful. Did one of his contacts come through?" She pulled out a chair and sat down next to her mother.

"Not exactly." Eleanor picked up her coffee mug and took a sip. "He's down at Wildheart Video—

they have an opening for a full-time clerk."

"Wildheart Video?" Courtney yelped, panicked because that's where most of her friends rented their movies. "What's he doing down there?"

"Applying for a job," Eleanor said calmly. "You know what a movie buff your dad is. What difference does it make where he's applying? A job's a job. At least if he lands this one he'll be doing something that actually interests him."

"But a video store clerk?" Courtney cried. "He only got laid off last week. Why isn't he trying for a good job?" She didn't understand any of this. Her father had worked in the computer industry for twenty years. Now he was applying for jobs at video stores. What was wrong with everyone? This was crazy.

Eleanor stared at her daughter, her expression a mixture of exasperation and sympathy. "Look, honey, I already told you not to get your hopes up that Dad's going to land another job like he had."

"I know what you told me," Courtney cried. "But just because there aren't a lot of good jobs around doesn't mean he should give up."

"He's not giving up. Dad's still going to be sending out résumés and networking with his old colleagues," Eleanor said patiently. "But times have changed. Whether we like it or not, we've got to do what we have to to survive. Frankly, I expected a little more maturity out of you about this. Your father feels lousy enough about losing his job—please don't make him feel bad if he manages to get this one. Besides, it's not like he's planning on doing it for the rest of his life. He's going to keep right on looking for another management job, but that may take awhile and in the meantime, we need to pay the bills."

Courtney clamped her mouth shut to keep the hot, angry words trapped inside. Her mother didn't understand. All her friends would see her father clerking behind the counter every time they went in to rent a movie. God, she'd be so humiliated. That cock-and-bull story she'd given Allison about her parents being in midlife crisis would only go so far. Everyone would see him. Everyone.

"Look, honey," Eleanor said gently, "I know this is hard for you. But it's hard for him too. It's tough on all of us."

"It isn't fair," Courtney cried. "Dad didn't do anything wrong. How come he had to lose his job?"

"Of course he didn't do anything wrong and of course it's not fair. But that's the way life is sometimes. There are no guarantees. Even the best-laid plans go off the rails, and when that happens you've just got to make the best of it." Eleanor reached over and patted Courtney's hand. "And Daddy and I are real proud of the way you kids have jumped in to help. Eric's got a job."

"Yeah, but I don't," Courtney moaned. "Nobody's going to hire me."

"It's early days yet," Eleanor said, laughing. "You've only been looking for a couple of days. That coffee shop was the first place you applied. There will be lots of other opportunities around."

"You and Eric got the first jobs you applied for," Courtney pointed out. It still niggled at her that she couldn't even land a part-time job in a greasy spoon on the wrong side of town. Part of her bitterly resented having to work, but another part of her just as strongly resented the fact that she couldn't find a job at all. She was scared. Underneath all the anger and the resentment was the fear. What if she couldn't ever find work? Her whole senior year would be a washout. She knew the family's financial situation. If she didn't work, there'd be no senior pictures, no clothes, no class ring, and no Winter Ball gown.

"We got lucky," Eleanor replied. "Let's keep our fingers crossed that your dad gets lucky with his interview today and that you find something soon too."

The phone rang. Courtney got up and answered it. "Hello."

"Hello, may I speak to Courtney Cutler, please," a deep male voice said. She knew instantly who it was. Her heart leapt into her throat and her heartbeat picked up a pace.

"This is she."

"This is David Nicks, from the Victorian Café," he said.

"Oh hi," she said, forcing herself to sound casual.

"I'm calling about the job," he continued. "If you're still available, I'd like to offer it to you."

She couldn't believe it. She was going to get the job. "Sure, I'm available. When do you want me to start?"

"Tomorrow afternoon," he said. "The afternoon shift starts at four. Will that give you enough time to get here after school?"

She'd be taking the bus and as she didn't have a clue how often they ran, she did some quick mental calculations and decided that she could make it. "That'll be fine. Uh, is there a uniform or anything?"

"No, the outfit you had on yesterday is fine. A white top and a dark skirt, but you might want to make the skirt just a little longer than the one you wore for the interview."

She could feel her cheeks flush. "Fine, I'll be there."

"Don't you want to know how much your pay is?" he asked, a note of laughter in his voice.

"Oh yeah," she smiled at her mom. "How much?"

"Minimum wage to start plus tips," he said. "We'll work out the rest of the weekly schedule when you get here. Bring a work permit and your social security card."

"All right, and thanks for giving me a chance," she said eagerly. "I know I don't have any experience, but I'm willing to give it my best."

"Well, to be perfectly honest," David told her with a laugh, "I usually don't hire inexperienced people. But I'm desperate. The only other person who applied was a biker mama who brought eight of her friends along for the interview. So let's hope this works out for both of us."

Deflated, she said, "Yeah, let's hope so."

She put the phone down and turned to see her mom grinning at her proudly. "Congratulations, kiddo. You did it!"

"Mom, it came down to me or a biker mama," Courtney said. She wished he'd hired her because he was impressed by her maturity or because he'd checked out her references and found out that she was a wonderful person.

"Who cares why he's hiring you?" Eleanor exclaimed. "You got the job, didn't you?"

"Yeah, but what if I'm no good at it?" Courtney voiced another fear that was plaguing her. "What if I'm clumsy or I don't catch on or I screw up the orders?"

"Don't be silly." Eleanor put her arm around her daughter's shoulders. "You're an intelligent, capable young woman. There's no reason to believe you won't do a fine job. Now quit worrying about what might happen and concentrate on what is happening. Remember, honey, most of life is just showing up and doing your best."

"Hey, anyone home?" her father's voice called from the front hall. A moment later, he appeared in the doorway to the kitchen. "How're my girls?"

"Fine. How did it go?" Eleanor went to her husband, her face anxious.

Jack Cutler grinned widely. "Went fine. I got the job. It's full-time too." He brushed a quick kiss on his wife's cheek and headed for the coffee pot on the counter. "At first the owner wasn't too thrilled with me. I think it was probably my age, but after we got to talking and he saw how much I knew about flicks, his whole attitude changed. The pay's not much, but it'll help keep the wolf from the door for a while."

"That's great, Dad," Courtney said. For the first time since he'd been laid off, he looked happy. She hadn't realized how much she'd missed his smile. "When do you start?"

"Tomorrow."

She laughed. "You're not the only one starting a new job tomorrow," she said proudly. "I got the job at the coffee shop."

He came over and gave her a big hug. "Congratulations. Looks like we have something to celebrate."

Celebrate? Courtney stared at her father. She didn't know how to feel. She was happy for him and for herself. But she felt weird too. Less than a week ago her dad had been a high-powered executive, now he was thrilled to be getting a job as a video store clerk. And she was thrilled to be getting a waitress job. She didn't understand. She didn't understand at all.

CHAPTER FOUR

Dear Diary,

I'm pretty nervous about this afternoon. Today I'm going to tell Allison and some of the other kids about the job. If I can just keep up the "my parents have flipped out" routine, I should be okay. The Victorian Café is hardly the kind of place they'll hang out at. Besides, if I can avoid it, I'm not going to be real precise about where I'm working. It would be just my luck for Hillary Steadman and a bunch of her creepy friends to come in and hassle me just for the fun of it. I'm not crazy about the idea of having to work, but I don't want to lose this job either.

Courtney tossed the diary into her drawer, quickly smoothed over the covers on her bed, grabbed her backpack, and headed out. Allison should be here any minute. She hoped Allison wouldn't be late. This morning she was going to hit the library before first period. She had a history paper due in less than three weeks and Courtney had the feeling that now that she was working, she couldn't afford to mess around until the last minute.

The day passed quickly at school. Allison hadn't asked a lot of questions about the job; she'd just smiled and told Courtney she hoped it would all work out. Courtney had been a little hurt. She'd only dropped cheerleading a week ago, but already her friend was so busy with her own life, she didn't seem to care much about what Courtney was doing. She knew it was silly to take it so personally. After all, she told herself as she hurried up to the bus stop, that was what she'd wanted—for her friends not to ask questions.

Courtney slung her backpack onto the bus bench. She glanced down at her outfit. She'd lengthened the navy blue skirt by a couple of inches, but if she was going to work more than one night a week, she'd have to buy a couple more skirts and blouses to wear to work. Strange how her wardrobe, extensive as it was, didn't run to many plain dark skirts and white blouses or T-shirts. She hadn't worn the outfit to school, but had tucked it into her pack and ducked into a restroom to change right after last period.

She frowned and craned her neck down the road, hoping she hadn't missed the three twenty bus. That's all she needed—to be late on her first day.

But she hadn't missed the bus, and all too soon she was getting off at the stop in front of the coffee shop. Taking a deep breath, she pushed open the door and stepped inside.

The blond waitress looked up from filling a tray of condiments at the counter. "Hi," she said, smiling. "So you got the job. Ready to get started?"

David came out of the kitchen, saw Courtney and nodded. "Good, you're on time."

Courtney stood there feeling awkward, her backpack still slung over her shoulder. "Hi," she murmured. The place wasn't exactly packed and she was glad. Maybe learning this job wouldn't be as hard as she thought.

"Lannie"—he nodded toward the waitress—"will show you where to clock in and stow your things. Then she can teach you how to do the tickets and what codes we use for the menu."

"Okay," Courtney muttered.

"I'll be in the office," he said, heading for the door on the other end of the waitress station. "You can pop in and fill out the rest of the new-hire paperwork as soon as you've put your stuff away."

"I hope you pick this up quick," Lannie said briskly as she turned and led the way down the counter, motioning Courtney to follow her. "I'm leaving in three days."

"Three days?" Courtney said. "You mean you're quitting?"

"Yup, My fiancée and I are moving to Las Vegas. He's in construction." She pushed through a set of double swinging doors at the end of the counter and led Courtney down a short hall. On one side was one of the entrances to the kitchen and on the other were a pay phone and a bunch of booster seats and high chairs jammed together. Beyond that was a row of battered metal lockers.

Lannie stopped at the end of the row, frowned at the lockers, and said, "Here, use this one." She pulled a key out of the lock and handed it to Courtney. "I'm not sure this lock works very well, but this place is pretty secure. None of the customers are allowed back here."

Courtney opened the locker and tossed her pack inside.

"Back here is where you clock in." Lannie led her to a small, cramped room just beyond the lockers and stopped in front of a clock. She pulled a time card out of a slot, one that had Courtney's name handwritten on the top, and handed it to her. "Just take the card and shove it in the top. It'll automatically clock you in. You clock in at the beginning of the shift and out again when you get off."

"What about breaks?" Courtney asked nervously, already terrified she'd make a mistake.

"We don't clock out for breaks," Lannie said and shrugged. "David's a decent boss. We work straight shifts."

"Uh, how old is he?" Courtney knew it was probably tacky to start asking questions about her supervisor right away, but she couldn't stop herself. "I mean, he looks so young to be a manager."

She laughed. "He is young, only nineteen. He's only the night manager. But he started working here when he was fourteen and he really knows his stuff. You ready to roll?"

Courtney nodded. She might as well get started. "Yeah, as ready as I'll ever be."

She stopped in the office and filled out the rest of her paperwork. Then, taking one last deep breath, she walked out onto the floor.

Lannie spent the first hour showing her where things were, teaching her how to make coffee, and introducing her to Henry, the cook, and Jorge, his assistant.

At six, just as the restaurant was starting to get

busy, another waitress came on duty. She was an older woman named Jewel, with dark, graying hair, a heavily made up face, and a ready smile.

"You'll do fine," Jewel said kindly as they were standing together by the register. "Just don't let anything rattle you."

But Courtney didn't do fine. Her first night was a disaster. By the time her shift ended, she'd broken a rack of glasses, spilled coffee all over the counter, and tripped over her own feet while carrying a hot plate. It was only sheer luck that the meat loaf special didn't end up on the kitchen floor. No one had said anything or yelled at her, but by the time she was clocking out, she was close to tears.

As planned, Eric was waiting for her at the bus stop. "How'd it go?" he asked eagerly.

Courtney blinked hard to stop herself from crying. She ducked her head and slung her pack on the bus bench, not wanting her younger brother to see her face. "Okay," she mumbled.

"You don't look okay," Eric said softly. "What happened? Did they can you already?"

"No, but it's only a matter of time," she said, bringing herself under control. "I probably won't last the week before they fire me."

"That bad, huh?"

"God, Eric, it was awful. No matter what I did, no matter how careful I tried to be, I kept screwing up. I broke a bunch of glasses—"

"Are they going to make you pay for them?" Eric interrupted.

She shook her head. "I don't think so. No one said anything."

"What else happened?"

"I spilled coffee all over the counter, messed up

two orders, and tripped over my own feet, almost dumping the blue plate special in the middle of the kitchen floor."

Eric smiled sympathetically and awkwardly patted her on the back. "Look, Court, did you do the best that you could?"

"Yes," she said earnestly. "I really did. I'll admit I'm not crazy about having to work—who is? But I tried. I really tried."

He stared at her a moment, his thin face grave. "It seems to me that if you did your best and you still screwed up, then maybe waiting tables isn't the job for you. But it's only one day. Give yourself a chance. Nobody's perfect right off the bat."

"But what if they fire me?" Courtney cried. "My boss didn't say anything, but I saw the way he was looking at me. He thinks I'm the clutziest thing on two feet."

"If you get fired, you get fired. Don't sweat it. The kind of jobs we have are pretty much at the bottom of the totem pole. There are plenty of others around."

"Let's hope so," she muttered, standing up as she saw the bus coming. "Otherwise I'm doomed."

But the next day, David didn't fire her. Nor the next day or the next. Courtney didn't know if it was because he was desperate for help or because she was actually catching on, but by the time Lannie left, Courtney was working the counter and feeling more comfortable with the customers. The tips there weren't as good as at the tables, but at this point, she was just grateful to be hanging on to her job.

Courtney managed to make it through the weekend. On Sunday she came home at six to find the house empty. Her father was working till ten at the video store, Eric was over at a friend's house surfing the Internet, and her mother was at the grocery store. She plopped down on the couch, kicked off her shoes, and stretched. Just as she was trying to find the energy to get up and get herself a soft drink, the phone rang. "Hello."

"Hi, kiddo," Allison said brightly. "Long time, no see. How's the job going?"

"They haven't fired me yet." Courtney said. "And the tips are okay—I've made over forty dollars so far. Another couple of weeks and I'll have the money for my senior class ring—" She broke off as she realized what she'd just said. This job was supposed to be about building her character, not earning money.

"What do you mean, you'll have the money for your ring?" Allison asked suspiciously. "Can't your parents pay for it?"

"Sure they can," she said quickly. "But paying for my own stuff is part of their 'build your character' routine." She crossed her fingers hoping she had carried off the lie successfully.

"Oh," Allison said. "Is that it?"

"Of course that's it," Courtney sputtered. "What do you think? That my parents are poor?"

"Hey, hey, take it easy," Allison said quickly. "No one said anything about being poor. Besides, there's no shame in that. But I was just wondering if that's all there is to it, that's all."

"I don't know what you mean."

Allison sighed. "Look, I'm not handling this right. It's just that all of a sudden, your mother's working at a nursery and you and your brother are both slinging hash. I just wondered if everything's all right, that's all. You know, if there's a problem, I'd like to help."

Sure you would, Courtney thought and then caught herself because she was being unfair. Allison was a good person. She might be from a rich family, but she had a kind heart, she always had. Yet Courtney still couldn't bring herself to tell her best friend the truth. "There's no problem except that my parents have gone into midlife crisis with a vengeance, that's all." She took a deep breath and plunged deeper into the abyss. "My dad's quit his job," she lied.

"Oh my God, he was serious."

"Very. He's gone to work in a video store. He says he's disgusted with the way corporate America is dehumanizing people. But if you ask me, he's just flipped out, some kind of male menopause or something." Courtney forced a laugh and waited. If she was lucky, Allison would believe her. Having her friends think her father was taking a social stand was a heck of a lot better than having people know the truth. That he'd been fired and couldn't find another job.

"Yeah," Allison said. "I think there's a lot of that these days. I think my dad has it too. He's been acting weird. He joined a gym, can you believe it? He's been working out and everything."

"That doesn't sound weird to me," Courtney said. "Maybe he's just trying to take care of his health."

"Oh sure, that's why he's dying his hair too," Allison sneered. "God, isn't there a hormone shot or something they can give them? Mom's menopause was bad enough. I didn't think I'd have to go through it twice. It's like all of a sudden he's trying to act like he's thirty-one, not forty-eight. It makes me sick, Court. Really sick."

Courtney was at a loss for words. She'd been so wrapped up in her own problems since school started that she hadn't even noticed that Allison might be down about something. But then again, she hadn't seen her friend all that much lately. "I'm sorry, Allison," she said softly. "How long has this been going on?" She wasn't sure that anything was going on, but Allison obviously thought there was.

"Since right before school started," she sighed. "He's lost twenty pounds, dyed the gray out of his hair, and started buying clothes that are way too young for him. I think he's having an affair."

"Come on, Allison," Courtney protested. She'd known Mr. Merrill since she was in first grade. He was a wonderful man. Kind, funny, and really devoted to his family. But, things could change. Courtney's life was living proof of that. "Don't go off the deep end here. Just because your dad's trying to look a little younger doesn't mean he's having an affair. Stop worrying about it, okay? Dying his hair and losing weight could mean he's scared of getting old, facing his mortality or something like that." She wasn't exactly sure what she meant, but she'd heard something like it on a radio talk show last week and it sounded good. Whether Mr. Merrill was having an affair or not, she didn't want Allison worrying about it.

"Yeah," she sighed again. "I guess I'm just a little uptight, that's all. Part of it is because it's so strange, not having you around all the time."

Courtney bit her lip. She wanted to rage that she was sorry too, but it wasn't her fault she had to work, it wasn't her fault she couldn't afford to be a cheerleader, and it darned well wasn't her fault that the bottom had dropped out of her life. But Allison wouldn't understand that. She wasn't sure she understood it herself. "I know. I miss you too. But what can I do? My parents are serious about me working. They said they're tired of me acting like a spoiled little rich girl sitting on her duff and waiting for the world to hand her everything on a silver platter."

"I know it's not your fault," Allison said quickly. "All I meant was that I miss you. Being on the squad isn't all that much fun without you. Geez, putting up with Hillary alone should qualify me for a medal."

Courtney laughed. "Consider yourself medaled, then. Besides, we see each other every day at school."

"But it's not the same." Allison denied. "Things have changed. I don't know, Court. Nothing's like it used to be. You're always working, my Dad's acting funny, and even being on the cheerleading squad isn't as much fun as I thought it would be. I don't think I like it now."

"Hey, don't say that," Courtney said quickly. "Nothing lasts forever. Things will go back to the way they were—they have to. Maybe I can't be on the squad, but one of these days, my parents will come to their senses, you'll find out your dad is just fine, and everything will be okay. Just wait, you'll see." But even as she said the words, Courtney knew they were a lie. She had a horrible feeling things would never be the same. But she fought that feeling back with the ferocity of a lioness defending her cub. *Things will change. My father will find a good job and then everything will be like it was.* She wouldn't have to work at the Victorian Café, her mom could give up that crummy job at the nursery, and she'd go off to Prior College with Allison. *Life will be fine, just fine,* she told herself as she hung up. All they needed was for her dad to get a decent break.

"How's the cake today, Mavis?" Courtney asked her favorite customer. She poured the elegantly dressed woman more coffee. Mavis came in every afternoon around four thirty. She had one slice of cake and coffee. Lots of coffee. Courtney wondered if all that caffeine kept the elderly woman awake at night. Perched like a brightly painted bird on one of the counter stools, Mavis Rand should have looked out of place sitting amongst all the truckers and deliverymen and taxi drivers that frequented the diner, but she didn't. With her perfectly coiffed dyed black hair, bright blue eyes, and ready smile, she fit right in. The other waitresses had told Courtney that Mavis used to be a costume designer in the movies and had come to Landsdale with her husband when they retired. But Mr. Rand was long gone. It hadn't taken Courtney long to understand that Mavis didn't come to the Victorian Café because of the quality of the cake, she came for the company. She was a regular and, by far, Courtney's favorite customer.

"Excellent, my dear." Mavis daintily dabbed at her mouth with her napkin, the diamonds on her hands sparkling as they caught the light. "I'm delighted to see you're more relaxed about working here. Frankly, my dear, when you first started, I was a tad concerned that you wouldn't last long."

Courtney laughed. She turned, put the coffeepot

back on the station, and reached under the counter for a damp dishtowel. "You weren't the only one," she admitted as she slapped the towel on the counter and began wiping the spot next to Mavis. "I didn't think I'd last long either, but David hasn't fired me yet."

"Of course he hasn't." Mavis giggled. "You're doing much better. Why, you haven't dropped a water glass or tripped over your own feet in days."

"Yeah, well, it was touch and go there for a while. But David was really patient with me; he gave me a chance to learn the ropes." Actually, from the scuttlebutt she'd heard around the kitchen, it wasn't that David had been all that patient. More like desperate. He hadn't exactly been deluged with applications for this job.

"He likes you," Mavis said in stage whisper loud enough for the whole restaurant to hear. Luckily, there weren't many people in the place.

Courtney's jaw dropped. "Are you kidding? I mean, uh, he's a nice boss and all that, but I don't think that means he 'likes' me or anything." She refused to let herself build up that hope. The truth was, David had fascinated her since the moment she'd laid eyes on him. She'd even stopped worrying about why Luke Decker hadn't called and asked her out again.

Mavis eyed her shrewdly. "Don't be silly, child. Of course he likes you—I can see it in his eyes every time he looks at you. Mind you, I don't think he'll ask you out. Not while he's your boss. David is a highly principled young man for one so young. He's had to be, you see. He practically started supporting his family when he was fourteen and his father died."

Courtney was dying to ask more questions, but she didn't want to get caught gossiping about the boss. She glanced over her shoulder. Henry was cleaning the grill pan and not paying any attention, Jewel was off filling salt and pepper shakers. Amy, the evening shift waitress, was out on the floor cleaning tables and David was in the back doing the weekly dairy order. "He supports his family?"

Mavis nodded earnestly. "Well, he helps. I believe the mother gets some Social Security," she explained, "but these days, that's never enough, and both David's sisters have got part-time jobs now, but they didn't when he first started working." She shook her head. "It's such a shame too."

"Yeah," Courtney agreed, "he sure didn't have much fun in high school."

"That's not what I meant," Mavis waved her hands dismissively. "I meant it was such a shame he had to stay here in Landsdale and go to the junior college instead of going off to San Diego, to that big university down there. He wants to be a marine biologist, you know. I expect he'll make it. David is quite a determined and focused young man. So very different from many of your generation."

"You mean the University of California at San Diego?" Courtney asked. "He got in there? And he couldn't go?"

"That's right, he had to stay here and work. Mind you, his mother wanted him to go, but they were having problems with his younger sister and David refused to go off and leave his mother to cope alone. But I expect he'll go next year. From what I've heard, Sandra—that's his sister—is doing quite well these days."

"Wow, that's really something," Courtney murmured. She didn't know what to think. David sounded like a saint. She cringed inwardly as she thought of her own resentments and anger because her father had lost his job. Jeez, David's father had lost his life.

"You could do worse than a young man like that," Mavis said bluntly. "There's something magic between the two of you. The very air seems to vibrate when the two of you are close together."

"Oh, come on, Mavis, the only reason he didn't fire me on my second day was because he was desperate for help. He's not in the least bit interested."

"Oh yes he is," Mavis insisted with a stubborn shake of her head. "You two are meant to be together. I can feel it. I can see it. Take my word for it, I know about things like that."

Magic? Right. Courtney laughed. Much as she wanted to believe Mavis, she didn't dare. David was just her boss. The only interest he had in her was whether or not she could pour coffee and carry hot plates.

By the time her shift ended, a light fog had drifted in from the coast. Courtney pushed open the door and stepped outside. As she wasn't working a late shift, her brother wasn't waiting for her. But still, Courtney looked carefully around before venturing out toward the bus stop. It might only be seven fifteen, but it was still dark. She slung her pack down on the bench and started to sit, then found herself jumping back, her hand still on the pack, as an old white Toyota pulled up alongside the curb.

"Hey," David yelled. "You want a ride?"

"I live over in Estes Park Estates," she said, bending down to peer in the open window. "Is that too far out of your way?"

"Hop in, I'll take you home."

She grabbed her stuff and climbed in the car, holding her pack on her lap.

"Dump that in the backseat," he said as he pulled out into traffic.

"Uh, thanks," she muttered, shoving her stuff in the back as she wondered why he was leaving this early.

She turned and straightened in the seat, pulled her seat belt on, and jammed it into the side slot. "Do you want me to give you directions?"

"I know where it is," he said, giving her a quick smile. "But once we're in the tract you'll have to guide me. How come you take the bus?"

"Because I don't have a car."

"Really? I thought all the kids like you had cars."

"What do you mean, 'kids like me'?" She found herself getting irritated. Not that he'd been sarcastic or anything. He'd asked the question matter-of-factly, as though it was no big deal.

"You know, kids from that part of town," he shifted gears and pulled into the left lane. "I didn't mean anything by it. I was just curious."

"Well, I don't have a car." She stared straight ahead, suddenly unsure of what to say or how to act.

"I know what that's like," he said. "I used to take the bus all the time myself. It's okay, except when it's cold or raining and then it's a real drag."

"Yeah, it is." God, she thought, that sounded lame. What was wrong with her? Had she become such a wussy she couldn't even make conversation? "Uh, how come you're not working tonight?"

"I'm taking the evening off," he said, shooting her another smile. "Henry's on duty, he can handle things, and I want to go to my kid sister's back-to-school night with my mom." He gave an embarrassed laugh. "Now, that sounds really lame, but there it is."

Courtney thought it sounded like just about the sweetest thing she'd ever heard. "I don't think it sounds lame at all. I think it's nice."

"What about you, got a hot date?"

She thought about it for a moment. Because she was getting off relatively early, she'd planned on going over to Allison's tonight. Some of the other kids were coming over and they were going to hang out. But her feet hurt and she was tired. Eric had mentioned something about bringing a pizza home with him tonight and she was having second thoughts. "Nah, I was going to go over to a friend's house. But I'm tired and I think my brother's bringing home a Gargantua Special, so I think I'll just stay home and read."

"What's a Gargantua Special?" David asked.

"The biggest, bestest pizza that Bongo Bongo makes," Courtney replied. Just the thought of it made her mouth water. "My brother works there and gets an employee discount."

"Is that the guy who meets you at the bus stop when you're on a late shift?" David asked.

Courtney slanted him a quick glance. She was surprised he'd noticed. "Yes, we worked it so we could take the bus home together when we work late. It's safer that way."

David nodded. "That's good. I kinda felt bad about putting you on Friday and Saturday nights when I realized you didn't have a car. You should have said something."

"I was afraid you wouldn't hire me if I said anything," she replied, "and I really wanted the job."

"Why?"

"Because I need the money," she said honestly. She was surprised at how it didn't bother her to say the words out loud. What was wrong with needing money? That's why people worked.

"Yeah, I hear that." He pulled onto the main street of the housing tract where she lived. "But if for some reason your brother can't meet you after you're working a late shift, I want you to tell me. Okay?"

"Why?" she asked suspiciously. "I mean, I know I don't have a car, but I'm not scared of taking the bus by myself. Uh, look, just because I have to take the bus doesn't mean I wouldn't be a reliable employee. . . . I mean, I wouldn't call in sick or anything like that. . . . I need this job. . . ."

"Hey, slow down," he said quickly. "I'm not going to fire you because you have to take a bus. I'm going to give you a ride home if you need it. Even in Landsdale, it's not exactly the safest thing to do, riding a night bus alone."

"Oh." She sagged against the seat in relief. For a few minutes there, she'd been sure he was going to use her transportation problems to can her. "That's really nice of you. Thanks. But Eric's real good about being there."

"Okay, but let me know if he can't be."

"Sure. Uh, sorry I jumped to the wrong conclusion, but like I said, I need this job."

"You saving for college?"

College? Courtney didn't have a clue about college anymore. "Sort of," she replied.

"What are you going to major in? Which street do I turn on?"

"Alvarado Drive, then a left at the first corner. We're the last house at the end of the block," she directed. "I haven't decided what I'm going to major in yet."

"What are you interested in?"

She thought about it for a moment. "Reading. I love to read," she finally replied, surprised because it was the truth. Since she'd been working, she'd actually started reading again. Mainly on the bus to work, but sometimes late on Friday or Saturday night when she got home from work too keyed up to sleep. "Maybe I'll major in English. How about you?"

"Marine biology," he said firmly. "I want to study whales. They've fascinated me since I was a kid."

"Do you ever go whale watching?"

"Every year," he said. "You?"

Courtney smiled. She hadn't been whale watching since she'd gone with her parents when she was ten. But maybe this year she would. Maybe the whole family should go. Stunned by the thought, she blinked. She couldn't believe it. Was she thinking that the Cutlers should go whale watching together? A family outing? Good grief, they hadn't done something like that in years. She must be more tired than she thought.

CHAPTER FIVE

Dear Diary,
  I don't know what to think about David. After he gave me that ride home a few weeks ago, I thought that maybe Mavis had been right and that he did kind of like me. But since then, nothing. Zip. Zero. No rides home, no little chats, no cute smiles, nothing. Now he's strictly business. He's the boss and I'm the employee. Maybe I imagined that ride . . . nah, that's not true, but maybe I read more into it than there really was. I'm good at doing that. Other than David, things are going okay, I guess. I don't have a lot of time to brood. Frankly, between work, school, and studying, I'm pretty busy. But on the up side, I've got a wad of cash saved for my senior year goodies and I've already picked out my class ring.

The telephone rang and Courtney frowned, wondering who would be calling her at seven thirty in the morning. She picked it up. "Hello."

"Hi, Courtney," Luke said cheerfully. "I hope I

didn't wake you. But I'm going on a field trip and I won't see you at school today. I wanted to ask if you wanted to go to a party with me on Saturday night."

Taken aback, Courtney hesitated. Luke hadn't asked her out in weeks. Rumor had it that he was dating Hillary Steadman. "Saturday night?"

"Yeah, you already got a date or something?"

"No," she replied cautiously. She wasn't sure she wanted to go out with him. But then again, why not? It wasn't as if David was falling all over her. "No, it's not that. I have to work. But," she added quickly, "I think I can get off early. What time?"

"I'd want to pick you up around eight. The party's over at Julie Proctor's place in Summerland. Her parents are going to Palm Springs for the weekend and that's just too good an opportunity to pass up."

"Okay, providing I can get the time off," she said, surprised at her own nerve. "I'll give you a call if there's a problem, okay?"

"Great, I'll see you Saturday night." He hung up.

Courtney stared at the receiver and shook her head. Why had she agreed to go out with Luke? *He is a nice kid but* . . . She paused and frowned. Luke was her own age—why did she think of him as a kid now? Maybe it was because now that she was working and being with people like Jewel and Amy and David for so many hours every week, she'd changed. But that idea made her uncomfortable. She hadn't changed. Well, not too much. Luke was a great guy, she should be pleased to be going out with him. Now all she had to do was convince Nelda, the new waitress, to trade shifts with her on Saturday.

Courtney didn't think about Luke until she walked into the Victorian Café later that afternoon.

Nelda was standing behind the register with David, so she didn't say anything except hello as she passed on her way to her locker in the back. She'd better ask David if it was okay before she asked Nelda to trade. But she didn't see why he should object. What did he care as long as the shift was covered?

She stowed her stuff in her locker, then flew into the bathroom and changed into her skirt and blouse. Grabbing a clean apron off the laundry cart, she hurried to the time clock and clocked in dead on at four.

"Just made it," David said, giving her a quick grin as he passed by.

"Could I talk to you a minute?" she called.

He paused by the door of the office. "Sure," he said, "come on in."

"I was just wondering if you'd have any objection to my switching shifts with Nelda on Saturday," she said as she walked toward the office.

David gazed at her thoughtfully. "You got a good reason?"

"Well," she began, not liking the way this was turning out, "I've kinda got plans and I thought that if Nelda didn't mind, that it wouldn't be a problem."

He looked down for a moment and then back up at her. "Sorry, Courtney, but I'd rather you didn't ask Nelda to switch shifts with you."

"Why not?"

"Because she'll say yes."

"But what's wrong with that?" Courtney asked. "It's not like I'm planning to do it every week. It's only this one time."

"Is it something really special?" he asked.

She shrugged. "It's just a party."

"A party?" He grinned. "Can't you go after you get off? Most parties last pretty late on a Saturday night."

"I've kinda been asked to go—you know, a date." She had no idea why she was reluctant to tell him, but she was. "If Nelda wouldn't mind switching, I don't see why you'd have a problem with it."

"But I do have a problem with it. First of all, Nelda's not experienced enough to handle the counter on a Saturday night. Secondly, it'll cost her money. She'll have to spend what little money she earns to hire a babysitter for that night," he explained. "Nelda's a single mother. She doesn't have child care in the evenings. She has to hire a sitter for evening shifts. That's why I've scheduled her for all day shifts."

"Oh." Courtney didn't know what to say. It didn't seem fair to her, but she didn't want to whine about it. "Okay, I won't say anything." She turned and started for the floor.

"Courtney," David called. "I'm sorry, I really am."

"It's okay," she mumbled. But it wasn't. She was really ticked off. She charged out to the floor and snatched up a coffeepot. She spotted Mavis sitting at her usual spot by the cash register. "Hi, Mavis," she forced herself to smile. "Ready for a refill?"

Mavis nodded eagerly. "What's got you so steamed up?"

Courtney stared at her. "I thought I was hiding it pretty good," she sputtered.

"Oh you are," Mavis agreed, "but I'm sensitive to atmosphere and when you walked out here, you brought a big black cloud with you. What's up? David giving you a hard time?"

"He won't let me ask Nelda to trade shifts on Sat-

NO GUARANTEES   77

urday night," she said, relieved to be able to get her
grievance off her chest. "It's not fair. I've got more
seniority than Nelda. Okay, not by much, I'll admit,
but jeez, all I wanted was one Saturday night off."

"Life generally isn't fair," Mavis said with a
shrug. "But I find that if you teach yourself to go
with the flow, everything works out in the end."

"Yeah, but you're not going to have to stand up
the most popular guy in school," Courtney muttered. "Everyone already thinks I'm a hermit these
days."

"You really like this young man?" Mavis asked.

Courtney opened her mouth to say yes. "No. But
it's the principle of the thing that ticks me off." She
caught herself and clamped her mouth shut. "Heck,
I meant to say *yes.*"

"No you didn't," Mavis challenged. "Or you would
have said it. You don't like this boy at all. You just
wanted to flex a little muscle and see where you
stood in the scheme of life. Well, dear, if you can't
go out with this young man, and I for one don't
think you ought to anyway, then the cosmos obviously has something better in store for you."

Courtney couldn't help it. She burst out laughing.
"Mavis, you're one of a kind."

"We all are, dear," Mavis said placidly. "Every
single one of us."

Courtney's chat with Mavis cheered her im-
mensely. By the time her shift ended she had a
pocketful of tips and for once, her feet didn't hurt.
She met Eric at the bus stop. He was uncharacter-
istically quiet that night. But when she asked him
what was wrong, he shrugged and just said it
hadn't been a good day.

At home, she went upstairs, counted her tips, and

took a quick shower. In her nightgown and bare feet, she went back down to find a snack. As she was passing the family room, she heard voices. She didn't know what made her stop, what made her stand quietly in the hall without announcing her presence. But some instinct kept her quiet. Peeking around the corner, she saw her mother sitting in the easy chair and Eric sitting on the couch. His tip money, changed as always into bills instead of coins, was spread out on the coffee table.

"Is this enough?" Eric asked, sliding the stack of bills toward Eleanor. "It's a week's worth, almost a hundred and twenty-five."

"Oh, honey," Eleanor sighed. "Of course it is. I just wish I didn't have to take it."

"Don't worry about it, Mom," he said. "It's not your fault."

"I promise I'll pay you back, sweetheart." Eleanor reached for the cash. "Once we get out from under this debt"—she waved her hands around the room— "I shouldn't have to take money from you."

"I said don't sweat it. I'm glad to help out."

Eleanor smiled at her son. "You do more than just help, honey. I don't know what we'd have done without you."

Eric got up. "I'm going to hit the hay, I'm beat. There's a big test in my trig class day after tomorrow and I want to get up early and study for it."

Courtney scurried back up the stairs and into her room. She waited till she saw Eric come up and go into his own room. Then she dashed across the hall and knocked softly on his door. "Eric," she whispered. "It's me. Can I come in?"

"It's open," he called.

She stepped inside and closed the door behind her. "Okay, what gives?"

Puzzled, he stared at her. "What the heck are you talking about?"

"Downstairs." She jerked her thumb toward the floor. "I saw you giving Mom your tips. How long has this been going on?"

"You really want to know?" he challenged.

She didn't, but not knowing would only make her feel worse. "Yeah, I really want to know."

"Okay, I've been giving Mom my tip money since I started working. That's what she buys the groceries with."

Courtney's eyes widened in shock. "Are you serious?"

"Is it something I'd kid about?" he replied.

She felt like she'd been punched in the gut. God, she'd known money was tight, but she hadn't realized it was this bad. They didn't even have money for groceries. This was unreal. This was what happened to people who gambled or drank or snorted cocaine up their nose. It didn't happen to people like them. "Why didn't you tell me?"

"Mom didn't want me to," he said honestly. "She thought that knowing how bad off we are would scare the crap out of you."

"It does," Courtney admitted dully. She wanted to collapse and roll up into a ball, hoping that this was all just a nightmare and that it would go away. But it wouldn't.

"Look, Court, forget I told you. Okay? There's nothing you can do about it. We'll get by." He yawned widely. "Go get some sleep. Things will look better in the morning."

But Courtney couldn't sleep. She tossed and

turned half the night. The image of her younger brother, the kid she used to look out for when they were little, giving all his hard-earned tips to their mother haunted her. Why hadn't they told her how bad things really were? Did her entire family think she was so selfish, so weak, that she couldn't handle the truth? Apparently so.

She opened her eyes the next morning and lay in her bed, staring at the ceiling. A dozen other questions flew in and out of her head. Questions she was afraid of asking. Questions she was afraid of not asking.

Slowly she got up, walked over to her dresser drawer, and pulled it open. Inside, neatly stacked in bundles of twenty-five dollars each, was all the tip money she'd earned since she started working. She'd put her paychecks in her bank account. But her tip money was all here. Three hundred dollars of it. Money she was saving for her class ring and senior pictures and a new dress for the Winter Ball. She stared at the bills for a moment then firmly closed the drawer.

She showered, dressed, packed her stuff up, and went downstairs. Eric had already gone to school and her father, having worked till midnight at the video store, was still asleep.

"Good morning, honey," her mother said as she opened the fridge and got out a carton of milk. "Do you have time for some cereal?"

"I'm not hungry," Courtney replied. "Uh, I'd like to ask you something."

Eleanor put the milk down on the counter. "Sure," she said slowly, "what is it?"

Courtney gathered her courage. She really didn't want to know, she really wished she didn't have to face this, but she couldn't not ask. "How bad are things? Please tell me the truth," she said. "I mean, I don't want you to sugarcoat it because you think it'll scare me. Not knowing scares me worse."

Her mother stared at her for a moment. "Okay, I'll tell you the truth. Things are pretty bleak. Even with your dad and I both working, we're not going to make it." She swept her hand in an arc. "The mortgage on this place takes every cent we both earn. That means there's nothing left to live on."

Courtney nodded. "So how are we paying our bills?"

"Eric's helping," Eleanor admitted. "Plus we've sold a few things. We sold the antique tallboy that was in my bedroom—that's paid the utility bills for the last couple of months—and your father sold his golf clubs, but frankly, we're running out of things to sell." She broke off and closed her eyes. "We didn't want to tell you until we had to, but we've already seen a realtor. We're putting the house on the market."

"We're going to sell the house?" Courtney said incredulously. She'd thought she was immune to any more shocks about their life, but she'd been wrong. "We can't. Where will we live? What would we do?"

"We'd do what thousands of other people do," Eleanor replied bluntly. "We'd either rent or buy a cheaper house. I'm sorry, honey, I know this isn't what you want to hear, but it's the way things are. Your dad and I are doing the best we can, but we can't go on much longer the way we are. If we don't sell this house soon, the bank's going to repossess it."

• • • •

"A little more coffee here, miss," the voice came from the other end of the counter.

Courtney started, grabbed the coffeepot, and hurried to refill Danny Ruckman's empty cup. "Sorry," she mumbled. "Looks like you've about run dry."

Danny, a repairman for photocopying machines and one of the Victorian's regulars, laughed. "It's okay, kid. I daydreamed a lot when I was your age too."

She smiled and went back to refilling the salt and pepper shakers. Daydreaming. She would have laughed only it wasn't funny. Daydreams were fun; being haunted by horrible visions wasn't. She picked up a half-empty salt shaker and twisted the lid off. From behind her, she could hear a sizzle as Henry slapped another burger on the grill. She'd been haunted all day by the image of Eric handing their mother his tips. If that wasn't bad enough, she was worried sick about losing their house.

"Hey, Courtney," David stuck his head out the door, "when you finish with the shakers, can you make sure the booths get wiped down good?"

"I was planning on doing that next," she told him, irritated that he'd reminded her. What did he think she was, an airhead? He'd told her about the booths when she came on duty today.

He smiled apologetically. "Sorry, I was afraid you'd forgotten. You've been in a fog since you came in." He disappeared back behind the door, leaving her alone with her thoughts.

Courtney finished the condiments and then went to get a pail of hot water and a clean dishtowel. As she wiped down the booths, she wondered what she could do. *Maybe,* she thought, leaning over and flicking some toast crumbs off the the vinyl seat, *maybe if I give my tips to Mom and Dad, we can keep the house.*

Then she thought of how hard she'd worked for that money and a wave of bitterness swept over her with the force of a hurricane. Courtney fought the ugly feeling off. *Getting angry won't solve anything,* she told herself firmly. Handing her tip money over just might pay a few of the bills, just might make the difference they'd need to keep going. So what if she didn't get a class ring or senior pictures. It was no big deal. From the gossip she'd heard at school, there were a lot of kids these days who couldn't afford goodies like that. Apparently her family wasn't the only one facing tough times. Considering how slim the order stack for class rings had been when she'd seen them in the office, she wouldn't be the only one with a ringless finger this year.

Courtney finished cleaning the booths and then made a pot of fresh coffee. Mavis would be in soon and she didn't want to give her the bottom of the pot.

The place began to fill up and Courtney was so busy, time flew by. By the time she finished her shift and got home that evening, she felt much better. She knew what she had to do.

"Hi, honey." Eleanor was in the foyer, taking off her sweater. "How was work?"

Courtney patted the pocket of her skirt and the sound of coins jingled. "It was a good tip day. Mom, can I talk to you?"

"Sure," Eleanor said. "But everyone's waiting in the kitchen. Eric brought home another Gargantua Special."

"This won't take long. Wait here." Turning, Courtney flew up the stairs and into her room. A few moments later she was back. "Here." She handed her mother the money she'd been saving. "Take it. I want to help. This ought to be enough to pay some utility bills and help with the groceries."

Eleanor stared at the money in her hand. When she looked up at Courtney, there were tears in her eyes. "Oh, honey, I don't want to take your money."

"Take it, Mom," Courtney insisted. "I'm a part of this family, you know. It's about time I pulled my share of the load. It's not fair for Eric to help and not me."

Eleanor blinked rapidly. "Are you sure? You were saving this for your ring and your pictures and a new dress—"

"I'll live without a class ring," Courtney interrupted. "As for the pictures, you and Dad have a decent camera. I'll get dressed up one day this year and he can take a whole roll of film. Come on." She grabbed her mother's arm. "Shove that money in your pocket and let's go eat. I'm starved."

Jack and Eric were already at the kitchen table. Eric was passing around paper plates and Jack was prying Cokes out of a six-pack. "How're my girls?" he called when he saw them.

"Hungry," Courtney replied. She noticed how much more relaxed her dad looked these days and wondered about it. You'd think with all their financial troubles, he'd be more stressed, not less. But that wasn't the case at all. He actually looked younger, happier. She glanced at her mother as they sat down at the table and noticed that Eleanor looked better too. Maybe it was the hair. Her mom used to wear it up in a tight French roll. Now it was held back in a casual ponytail, with cute little wisps framing her face. Or maybe it was the clothes. Since taking the job at the nursery, Eleanor now favored jeans and shirts instead of dresses and pantsuits. Whatever it was, Courtney decided as she reached for her soft drink, both of them looked a heck of a lot better than they used to.

"How was work?" Courtney asked Eric.

Eric grinned. "Loose Change was in today. He bought two specials to go."

"Who's Loose Change?" Eleanor asked curiously. She reached over and helped herself to a slice of pizza.

"He's our current candidate for Crazy of the Year," Eric replied around a mouthful of pizza. "He refuses to use bills—you know, ones, tens, twenties."

"You mean he pays with a credit card?" Jack asked. "Lots of people do that. People even rent videos on credit cards."

Eric shook his head. "No credit cards either, he claims they're dangerous. He spent ten minutes the other day telling me how aliens—and I don't mean people from foreign countries—are using the magnetic strip on credit cards to track us."

Eleanor giggled. "How does he pay, then?"

"With quarters." Eric said, laughing. "The manager just about comes unglued. The guy comes in twice a week, orders two of the most expensive pizzas in the place, and then shells out nickles, dimes, and quarters to pay for them. Working with the public has been a real eye-opener. It sure takes all kinds."

"Tell me about it," Jack groaned. "You should see some of the weirdos that come into my store. There's one woman who rents the same film over and over again. Finally I said, 'Look, why don't you buy a copy? It would save you a lot of money.' But she didn't want to, claimed it was more fun renting the darned thing."

"What movie is it?" Courtney asked curiously.

"*The Terminator*. You should see this woman—she's eighty-five and looks like a Norman Rockwell painting of someone's grandmother." He laughed. "But she's a nice lady, even if she is a bit weird. Actually, I think she likes to come in because of the company, so I always take a few minutes to chat with her."

"Oh," Eric said, "that reminds me. Tony said to say thanks to you for recommending that movie."

Jack stared at him blankly. "Who's Tony?"

"One of the other kids who works at Bongo Bongo," Eric explained. "He comes into your store all the time. I'm sure you know him. He's short with red hair and always rents a science fiction movie."

"Oh, him." Jack's face brightened in recognition. "Nice kid. He was complaining the other day about there not being enough sci-fi movies and I recommended he see some of the old classics."

Eleanor rolled her eyes. " 'Classics'? Really, honey, I know you're a movie buff and a science fiction fan, but I can't honestly think of any old sci-fi movies that could be called classics."

"What about *2001* or *Forbidden Planet* or the original version of *The Thing*? You can't tell me those aren't classics," Jack argued.

"Okay, I'll give you the first two," Eleanor agreed. "But I'm drawing the line at *The Thing*."

"And they're off and running," Eric intoned in a singsong as their parents entered a good-natured argument over classic movies. But everyone knew that Jack would be the hands-down winner; movies had been his hobby since he was ten.

By the time they'd finished dinner a good half hour later, the whole family was involved in the discussion. As Eric and Jack had set the table, Eleanor and Courtney thought it only fair that they should clear up.

"Cool," Eric shouted as he raced for the stairs. "I want to study some more for that trig test."

"How are your grades doing?" Eleanor asked Courtney. But for once, her tone wasn't accusatory, merely matter-of-fact.

Courtney dumped the last of the dirty paper plates in the trash. "About the same—B's and C's. My job isn't taking all that much time away from my homework."

Eleanor looked down at the table. "I know," she said softly. "Your dad and I are very aware that it's your social life that's gone kaput. The other day I heard you on the phone telling Luke Decker you couldn't go out with him because you had to work. You shouldn't have to give up your social life, especially in your senior year. But honestly, Courtney, I don't know what we can do. Daddy didn't plan on losing his job and not being able to find another one that paid anywhere near what he used to earn."

Courtney glanced at her sharply. Was she hearing right? Was her mother actually saying she didn't socialize enough? But as soon as she saw the expression of pain on Eleanor's face, she knew she'd heard correctly.

"Hey, it's okay," she said, forcing her voice to be casual. "I went out too much before. Half the time I only went somewhere because I didn't have anything else to do. Don't worry about me not going out

with Luke. I didn't really like him all that much
anyway."

As soon as she said the words, Courtney realized
it was the truth. Calling Luke and canceling their
date hadn't been the high point of her week, but he
was hardly heartbroken. He'd taken it well. But
she'd known that he would never ask her out again.
That didn't bother her either. Lately, she'd found
her taste in the male of the species had radically
changed. The tall, lanky, serious type was more her
style. Too bad the candidate she had in mind happened to be her boss.

Eleanor stared at her for a long moment. "Well,"
she finally said. "I still wish things could be different. But they're not and we've got to live with the
world as it is, not as we want it to be." She smiled
suddenly. "Thanks for the money, honey. I'll keep
track of every cent you give me and one day, I'll pay
it back. If we can sell the house quickly, I may be
able to pay you back before you graduate."

"Mom, do we really have to sell the house?"

Eleanor nodded sympathetically. "We wouldn't if
we didn't have to. As a matter of fact, it may sell
before it even hits the market. The realtor we
talked to, well, we didn't call her, she called us. She
actually already had someone who was interested.
It seems the prospective buyer went completely
bonkers over the front yard." She sighed. "I'm sorry,
sweetie, but even if we don't sell it to this buyer,
we've got it priced to sell quickly."

"What about if I gave you my paycheck as well as
my tips?" Courtney suggested hopefully. If they had
to move, no one would believe that cock-and-bull
story about her parents flipping out because of midlife crisis. But that wasn't what was really moti-

vating her—Courtney was pretty sure that Allison and a couple of her other friends weren't buying that number anyway. Her true motivator was simple: She didn't want to lose her home. She'd lived here for as long as she could remember. Her parents had moved to this tract when it was first built. "Would that make a difference?"

"I wish it would," Eleanor said gently. "But it won't. This place costs a fortune to run. It's not just the mortgage, honey. We've got a second and the property taxes and the homeowners' association. It's a whole load of debt that we have to get out from under if we're going to survive."

CHAPTER SIX

November 30th

Dear Diary,

I'm sitting on the floor in my empty room. That's right, empty. All my furniture, clothes, and everything else was loaded into a moving van at the crack of dawn this morning. My parents not only sold the house fast, they must have had the shortest escrow on record. The prospective buyers not only wanted the place, they had a wad of cash to buy it with. Before I knew what had hit me, the house was sold.

I haven't even seen the new place. Why should I? We're losing our home, we're poor, and the rest of my family is carrying on like it's some big adventure. Mom and Dad have taken something called a lease-option on a house over on Twin Oaks Blvd. Can you believe it? Twin Oaks Boulevard! That's practically the ghetto. And they're pissed because I'm not enthusiastic. Well, excuse me, but I'm just dying to tell all my friends that we had to sell our home and now I'm living in a ghetto. Yeah, right.

Courtney tossed her pencil down and stared around the empty room. The new owners were moving in tomorrow. They had a daughter a little younger than her. She wondered how the girl would like living in her house, in her room. Tears welled up in her eyes, but she fought them back. She'd already indulged in a couple of good self-pity bouts; there was no point in doing it again. No matter how much she cried, it wouldn't change things.

From downstairs, she heard the vacuum cleaner switch off. Courtney got to her feet. They'd be leaving soon. Slowly she headed for the door, stopped, took one last look at the room she'd grown up in, and then walked out.

In the car, Courtney sat quietly in the backseat. Eric was sitting next to her, balancing a carton of books on one knee and his boom box on the other. The day was gray and overcast, matching her mood precisely.

"We're almost there," Eleanor said enthusiastically. Jack pulled around the corner onto Twin Oaks Boulevard. This part of the boulevard was residential. Courtney peered out the window. The houses, old California bungalows and Victorians, weren't quite as run-down as she'd thought. Most of them were nicely painted with well-kept yards and neatly mowed lawns. Her father drove to the end of the block, where Twin Oaks crossed with Poplar, and pulled into the driveway of the last house.

Courtney didn't look until she had to. She got out of the car and lifted her head. She bit her lip. It was worse than she'd expected. Dull gray and badly in need of a paint job, the huge, two-story Victorian sat back off the street. The stairs and the wide front porch had once been white, but were now coated with a layer of grime. She did notice, though, that none of the windows were cracked or broken and at least the porch didn't sag.

"Well, this is it," her father announced. He grinned at her and headed for the front door. "Come on, honey," he yelled to his wife. Eleanor, who'd stopped to poke around in the flower beds bordering the front of the yard, laughed and ran to join her husband.

Her mother, still giggling like a schoolgirl, ran up on the porch. Jack had the door open by this time and, to Courtney's utter amazement, he scooped her mother up in his arms and carried her over the threshold.

"Good grief," she muttered. "Look at those two. They're acting like a couple of lovebirds."

"I think it's kinda neat," Eric said, grinning at her. "In case you haven't noticed, they've been kind of lovey-dovey a lot lately. Come on, let's give them a few minutes to themselves in the house. There's something in back I want to show you."

Dutifully, Courtney followed him around the side of the house and into the backyard. She stopped and blinked in amazement. It was huge! Two gigantic maple trees stood like sentinels in the middle of the lawn. Piles of leaves were everywhere. Flower beds filled with weeds and overgrown bushes bordered a tall wooden fence that surrounded the property and what looked like the remains of an old vegetable garden filled in the ground between the trees and the fence. Catty-corner to the back porch was a small shed. "Geez," Courtney sputtered. "Look at this mess."

"Just give Mom a few months," Eric said. "She'll

have it looking like a showplace." He pointed to the bare-branched maples. "Those trees'll come in handy next summer when it's hot."

"Yeah, but who's going to rake all these leaves now?"

"Don't have hysterics, Court. It's only a few leaves. Come on, I want to show you the shed." Eric grabbed her arm and tugged her in that direction. He unlocked the door and stepped inside.

Expecting the worst, she followed him in. But the place was clean, swept bare, with a concrete floor and plain wood walls. "Okay," she said, "what's the deal? You going to live out here?"

"Nah, this is going to be my woodworking shed." He flicked on the lights. "See, there's electricity and everything. I've always wanted to do woodworking, you know, make furniture and stuff. Now I can. This is gonna be so cool. Donovan Richter's dad has a couple of used saws and some other equipment he's going to sell me. I've got some tools. I can pick up a bench and a couple of sawhorses over at the hardware store. Man, I can't wait. No way could I have done this at the old house. This is perfect."

Courtney stared at him incredulously. "You like this place? This house? For God's sake, we're practically going to be living in a ghetto."

"Don't be so melodramatic," Eric snapped. "Landsdale doesn't have a ghetto. Okay, this neighborhood isn't like our old one, but it's a good neighborhood. Mom's just itching to get at the gardens and Dad's so relieved he doesn't have that huge mortgage and second hanging over his head, he practically tap-danced on the front lawn. What's buggin' you?"

"What's bugging me?" she echoed. "Geez, we've

just lost our house, we're working our butts off, and now we're living in this dump. Gee, Eric, I don't know what's wrong. Maybe I'm just having a bad hair day."

Eric stared at her and shook his head. "Okay, I know this isn't your first choice in housing."

"It's a dump," she cried, blinking to hold back the tears. "I'm going to die if my friends find out. How can I bring them here? God, I'll bet the inside looks even worse than the outside."

"It's clean," he said quietly. "But it needs redecorating. You know, C.C., maybe things would be easier if you'd just tell everyone the truth. We're not the only ones at school who've had the wind knocked out of them. Lots of kids don't have much money anymore. In case you haven't noticed, the student parking lot isn't all that full these days."

Courtney shook her head and swiped at the tears spilling down her cheeks. "No, I won't do that. Not yet." She sniffed. "Come on, let's go inside. Don't worry, I won't spoil things for Mom and Dad by complaining. But don't expect me to tap-dance on the floorboards, either."

Eric had been right, the inside of the house was clean, but that was the best you could say for it. Courtney stood at the bottom of the staircase and frowned at the worn gray carpet leading up to the second story. Dark wood paneling, once bright and shiny but now dulled with age, climbed halfway up the hall wall. She wandered into the living room. It was huge, with high ceilings, old-fashioned wall sconces, the same dull paneling as the hall, and faded gold-and-green wallpaper. The same ugly gray carpet was in here as well. Slowly, she toured the rest of the house. But her mood didn't improve.

The kitchen was huge and in bad need of a paint job. There was a full dining room, also in need of refurbishing, a family room, a utility room off the back porch, and another small sitting room. Courtney shook her head and glanced back up the stairs. She didn't think the odds were good that the upstairs would be in any better condition, but she had to face it at some time or other.

She stomped up the stairs, stood in the open door of the room that was going to be hers, and grimaced. Except for the fact that it had a high ceiling and was shaped in a huge octagon, her room was as dull and ugly as the rest of the place. But there was a window seat. Drawn to it, she wandered over and sat down. The view looked out on the backyard.

She sat there for a long time, listening to the moving men as they started unloading the furniture. Her brother's words kept playing over and over in her head. Finally, the movers came to her room. She got up. She located her backpack and pulled out a clean skirt and white blouse. Even today, she had to go to work.

"This is my new address," Courtney sat on a chair opposite David and shoved a piece of paper across the desk. "We moved today."

His dark eyebrows rose in surprise. "Moved?"

"We sold the other house," Courtney explained, even though he hadn't asked. "The mortgage on it was killing us. My dad lost his job a few months ago and we just can't afford that kind of place anymore." For some reason, telling David the truth wasn't like telling her friends at school. Instinctively she knew he wouldn't laugh or sneer at her.

"I thought your father worked at that video store over on Main."

Now Courtney was surprised. She'd never told David where her father worked. "How'd you know that?"

He shrugged and looked a little embarrassed. "Uh, your brother must have mentioned it."

"You know Eric?"

"Well"—he actually blushed—"sometimes I go into Bongo Bongo for a pizza on my way home. Like you, I get awfully sick of fried food. I happened to mention to Eric that, uh . . . we worked together and, well, we've talked a few times."

A few months ago, Courtney would have cringed at the idea of her brother talking to a guy she liked, but these days, she and Eric had become pretty close. She knew Eric wouldn't say anything to hurt or embarrass her. Not intentionally, anyway. "Eric never told me he knew you."

"I'm sorry about your dad, losing his job, I mean." David smiled slightly. "There's a lot of that going on these days. I know what's it like to have the wind knocked out of your sails. It was like that for us when my dad died. One day we were an ordinary middle-class family, the next, we were poor."

Courtney sat perfectly still, waiting for the shame and humiliation to come. But it didn't. Instead, she felt relief. "The only job my father could find was at that video store," she continued, "but he really likes it. He earned a lot of money at TechniQuik, but I don't think he liked it much. But his leaving there's really changed our lives. All of us have to work now, just to make ends meet."

"Tell me about it," David said, laughing. He glanced down at the paper and his smile widened.

"Looks like you've moved into my neighborhood."

"You live near me?"

"Just around the corner, on Poplar." He leaned back in his chair. "Has your phone number changed?"

"No, it's still the same." She only wished he'd call her once in a while for something other than covering someone else's shift.

Allison sighed deeply and brushed a lock of hair out of her eyes. She leaned forward, shoving her lunch tray out of her way. They were in the senior quad at Landsdale High—Courtney, Allison, Jackie Dover, and Suzanne. "What time do you get off work tonight?" Allison asked Courtney.

"It's my day off," Courtney said. She'd been staring blankly across the quad, tired from all the unpacking she'd done this weekend. Between work and getting her clothes in some kind of order, she hadn't gotten much sleep. She only hoped that this afternoon her teachers wouldn't expect too much from her.

"Good, I haven't seen you in weeks. Can I come over?"

Courtney's head jerked around. For a moment, she started to make up an excuse. Allison hadn't picked her up this morning. Courtney had called and said she was getting a ride in with her mother. It wasn't a lie—she had gotten her mom to drop her off. But only because she hadn't wanted Allison to see where she lived. Suddenly she couldn't stand it anymore. How long could she keep this up? More importantly, why did she have to? She hadn't done anything wrong. There was no reason to skulk around like a criminal. She glanced around at the faces of the other girls at the table. These were her friends. If they didn't understand, then were they really worth keeping? Or worrying about?

"Sure you can come over." She smiled broadly and flipped open her notebook. "I'd better write my new address down for you."

"You've moved?" Allison cried. There was a collective gasp from the other girls. "But when? Why didn't you say something?"

Courtney held up her hand. She was taking a big risk here, but she couldn't stand living a lie anymore. It was just too darned hard. "Maybe I'd better explain. You see, my dad didn't go into midlife crisis in September. He got laid off." Without giving herself time to think, she plunged on and told them everything.

"Wow," Jackie said when Courtney had finished. "You're helping to support your family?"

"Well, I'm not helping all that much," Courtney admitted, searching their faces, "but I do pay the utility bills and help with the groceries. At least I did until we sold the other house. Now my parents don't need it so much."

"Why didn't you tell me before?" Allison asked softly. "I knew something was wrong."

Courtney sighed. "I was embarrassed. It's so hard, you know."

"I know what you mean," Suzanne interjected. She smiled at Courtney. "I thought about doing the same thing when my dad got laid off, but since the only job I could get was right under everyone's nose, I knew I couldn't pull it off."

"But at least you weren't dumb enough to try and live a lie," Courtney said.

"No, but I probably would have if I'd thought I

had half a chance of getting away with it. Dumb, huh? But that's the way you feel. Like you've done something wrong."

"Did you think we'd all dump you just because of something like that?" Allison asked. "I'm your best friend, couldn't you have told me?"

Courtney reached over and put her hand on Allison's arm. Her friend's face was flushed with anger. "I almost did," she said honestly. "And no, I didn't think you'd dump me. I know you're not that shallow. But you don't know how scary it is to have your whole world turned upside down. You don't know what it's like to come home one day and find out that everything you thought was permanent in life has disappeared. Besides, I didn't want anyone's pity. I wanted everyone to still accept me as an equal."

"My dad's job is pretty shaky," Jackie said after a moment. "It's all my parents talk about." She gave Courtney a wan smile. "If he gets laid off, I don't know what we'll do. We don't have any money saved either. It takes every cent my dad earns to pay the bills. Who knows"—she laughed shakily—"I might be down at the Victorian Café applying for a job myself soon."

"Let's hope he doesn't get fired, then," Courtney said brightly. "But if it does happen, it's not the end of the world."

"It's not fun," Suzanne added, "but it won't kill you. My father's still trying to find something, but with my mom and me both bringing in some cash, we've made it. Of course, we've never lived in a big house either." She looked down at the address Courtney had scrawled in her notebook. "I only live a couple of blocks from you."

"What's the neighborhood like?" Courtney asked.

"It's pretty cool." Suzanne shrugged. "Not as fancy as the housing tract you're from, but it's safe and everyone knows everyone. It's one of the old neighborhoods. A lot of people who live around there have been there for a long time. It's a real mix, though."

"A real mix?" Allison said. "What does that mean?"

"It means that it's not lily-white and boring," Suzanne said with a wide grin.

Courtney's friends didn't come over that day. After hearing that the family hadn't even had time to unpack everything because of all their crazy work schedules, they'd decided to wait awhile to give the Cutlers time to settle in.

Courtney, who now felt as though the weight of the world had been lifted off her shoulders, cheerfully unpacked, cleaned, put away, and tidied up. Once their own furniture was in, curtains hung, pictures and photos on the walls, and their knick-knacks and personal possessions strewn about the rooms, the house seemed much more like home.

It was about two weeks after her announcement that the girls did drop by after school. Courtney wasn't scheduled to work until seven so she had plenty of time to give her friends the grand tour. She was nervous.

"Uh, it's not like the other place we had," she explained as she led them up the stairs to her room. "We haven't had time to do anything but unpack. Mom hasn't had the time to even think about redecorating." She didn't tell them that their mother was so in love with planting her English garden in both the front and the backyards that she hadn't said a word about redecorating and probably wasn't going to. Eleanor Cutler spent every spare second she had outside. If you stood still for thirty seconds, she'd bore your ears off with details about soils, mulch, plants, and the snail conspiracy to ruin her flower beds. But Courtney had never seen her mother so happy, so she kept her mouth shut.

But oddly enough, none of the girls commented on the ugly colors, the dark paneling, or the faded carpet. They were all wildly enthusiastic about the house.

Suzanne was crazy about Courtney's bedroom. "I'd kill to have a real window seat," she said as the girls trooped down into the living room.

"I like this room," Jackie added. "You could hold a barbecue in here without it being crowded."

"You've got a lot of potential here," Allison said, glancing up at the high ceiling. "This could be a real showplace if you wanted."

"Uh, Courtney," Eric interrupted from the doorway. "David's on the phone."

"Maybe he's finally going to ask you out," Allison hissed as Courtney hurried past her toward the phone in the hall. Courtney shot her a warning look, hoping the other girls hadn't overheard. Allison was the only one of her friends who knew how much she liked David and Courtney wanted to keep it that way. David, despite all her wild fantasies, was still all business with her.

Courtney hurried out to the hall to take the call. She came back a few minutes later. "Sorry, girls, but I've got to cut out now. My boss needs me to come in early today."

Her friends left and she dashed upstairs to get

dressed. When she came back down, Eric was waiting for her at the foot of the stairs. "I might as well go in with you," he said.

"I thought you didn't have to be in until five," she said, grabbing her purse and jacket.

"I want to stop at Donelly's Hardware Store on Jackson Street," he said, holding the door open for them both.

They started up the street toward the bus stop. One of the few good things about moving here, as far as she was concerned, was that their bus ride was now much shorter.

"Why?" Courtney asked idly. "Do you need more tools?" Eric had put his woodworking shop together with a speed that had amazed her. "It looks to me like you've got everything under the sun in there."

"I want to check out a few things," he said. "You've got to admit, it's great having a little money."

One of the other nice things about moving was that now both of them could keep most of what they earned. Their mom and dad didn't need their tip money to pay the bills since their mortgage payments had been slashed in half. Courtney didn't kid herself that the family was out of the woods yet, but they were doing lots better. "Yeah," she agreed. She plopped down on the bus bench and peered down the street to see if the bus was coming. "I'm saving all my tips. If I do get asked to the Winter Ball, I want to be able to buy a decent dress."

Eric sat down next to her. "Who do you want to ask you?"

A few months ago, Courtney would have died before she'd have ever confided anything to Eric. But things were different now. They'd actually almost become friends. "Well," she said slowly, "I'd love for David to take me, but that's not going to happen. So I guess I'd go with anyone. I really want to go. I've missed a lot of things this year and I'd hate to miss out on this too."

The next afternoon Courtney came home from school and dumped her backpack on the table in the hall. She went upstairs to change into her work clothes. Then she hurried back down, trying to find her brother. She checked the living room first, though usually if Eric had a free half hour before work, he was out in his workshop. But she was in luck. He was sitting in front of the TV. "What time is Mom coming home?"

Eric didn't answer. Courtney sighed. "Earth to Eric," she sang out. "Acknowledge."

"Huh?" He looked at her and grinned. "Sorry, I was concentrating. What did you say?"

"When's Mom due home? Should I take a pound of hamburger out of the freezer, or did she remember to get something out this morning?"

"She asked me to bring home a pizza," he asked, his gaze once more turned to the TV. "Since it's Friday, Dad won't be home till late and she's working till eight."

"Till eight? Why so late?"

"One of her customers is dropping by to ask Mom to look over a landscaping plan. Seems Mom's boss is real impressed by her and asked her to stay late to talk to these people."

"So we'll be eating together."

"Yeah, but it'll be late. After ten at least by the time you and I get home."

"Okay," Courtney said. She hadn't seen much of

either of her parents this week. A meal together would be nice. "Hadn't you better get ready? We've got to get going if we don't want to be late."

"Just a minute. I want to see this."

"What is it?" Courtney asked. She glanced at the TV. It was one of those home improvement shows. "What are you watching?"

Eric jumped up and flicked off the television. Turning, he rushed over to one corner of the huge room, edged a chair aside, and dropped to his knees.

"What the heck are you doing?" Courtney asked.

"Pulling up the carpet." He grunted as he yanked up the tacked end of the rug. "See, we've got hardwood floors under here." He pulled it farther back. "And from what I can see, it's in great condition."

"I don't care if it's polished black marble," Courtney retorted. "We have to get to work. I can't afford to be late. David will have my head."

"Don't sweat it," Eric muttered, squinting at the exposed floor. "You could probably get away with murder. David likes you."

"Right," Courtney snorted. But she wondered all the same. Eric and David did talk to each other. Maybe David had said something.

Eric stood up and gave her a broad grin. His eyes were twinkling. "Come on, let's go. We can talk on the bus."

"Talk about what?" she asked suspiciously.

"About Mom and Dad's Christmas present," he said.

They timed the bus perfectly. Eric wouldn't say another word until he and Courtney were settled in their seats by the back door.

"Okay, what gives?" Courtney said. "What's all this about Christmas presents? I thought at the last family powwow that everyone agreed to keep things simple."

"Define simple."

"Like under twenty bucks each for presents," Courtney replied. "And you know it."

"You know I'm good with my hands," Eric said. "I really like puttering around and doing things in the house, right?"

"So? What's that got to do with cheapie Christmas presents?"

"So I was thinking that this year, instead of a tie that Dad won't wear and a bottle of Chanel that'll gather dust on Mom's dressing table, we ought to give them something they'd really like. It wouldn't be just their present, either. It would be to ourselves too."

"Such as what?" Courtney peered at her brother suspiciously. He was up to something.

"Such as redecorating the house."

Courtney blinked. "Are you kidding? How the heck could we do that?"

"It's easy. I'm not talking about ripping out walls or tearing down ceilings," Eric exclaimed. "Just a little paint and wallpaper. It'll be a breeze—any idiot, even *you,* can slap paint on a wall."

"Gee, thanks."

He waved his hands impatiently. "I didn't mean it like that. But we could do this. Our house is really neat, even your friends think so."

"Were you eavesdropping?" Courtney glared at him. Eric hadn't done that since he was fourteen and decided that she and her friends were boring.

"Eavesdropping?" he said laughingly. "I didn't have to. Suzanne and Jackie are so loud you could probably hear them all the way to the mall. But that's not the point, we could really make that place look good. Mom and Dad would love it. They're too busy to do it. Mom's too busy with her garden and Dad's all thumbs."

"Aren't you forgetting something?" Courtney said. "First of all, we can't afford it and second of all, we don't have time. In case you haven't noticed, between work and school we're pretty much tied up."

"We both get Sundays off," he pointed out. "And with my expertise and you as gofer, I figure we could do a whole room in one day. I'm good at this kind of stuff, C.C., I really am."

"I know that," she said slowly. The idea was beginning to appeal to her. Eric was good with his hands. "But what about the expense? Even paint and wallpaper cost money."

Eric shrugged. "No sweat. My tips have been good lately. I'll pay for it. All I want from you is labor. You know, blood, sweat, and tears."

"I don't know, Eric," she said. But the idea of living in a house that was beautiful had taken hold of her. It wasn't so much that she cared what anyone else thought—and that was a bit of a surprise for her. It was more that she'd like to see what that old wreck could look like. "What about the paneling? Won't that have to come down? I mean, that's a big job."

"We'll leave it up."

"But it's ugly," she protested.

"Only because it hasn't been stripped and shined," he said confidently. "Come on, say yes. I can't do this on my own."

"But I'm saving for my dress . . ."

"I told you, I'd spring for the supplies."

"That wouldn't be fair."

"Come on, say yes. You know you want to," he cajoled.

"Yeah, but I really do need to save my money—"

"You don't even know that you're going to get asked to the Winter Ball," Eric interrupted. "Besides, if you do get asked to the ball, you can rent a dress."

"Rent one?"

"Sure, there's a place over on Santos Road that rents tuxes—you know, for prom night and stuff like that. You can rent dresses there too. I saw one in the window. Bright pink and white froufrou thing. It had one of those full skirts and a couple hundred yards of red lace around the bottom. You'd love it."

Courtney didn't have time to dwell on David for very long. By the time Mavis left, the place was filling up with the dinner crowd. She ran her legs off carrying chicken-fried steak and homemade stew back and forth along the counter. When her shift ended, she grabbed her backpack and hurried out to the bus stop to wait for her brother.

Eric arrived just as David's car pulled up in front of the stop. "Want a ride home?" he called.

"Are you sure it's no trouble?" Courtney asked.

"It's on the way, remember?" he said, reaching over and unlocking the passenger door. Eric got in first and climbed into the backseat. Courtney took the front.

"Thanks for the lift," Eric said. "It sure beats taking the bus."

"No sweat." He looked over at Courtney and smiled. "I hear the two of you are going to be doing some fix-it work around the house."

"How'd you hear that?" she asked. David had been in the office when she'd been talking about Eric's idea to redo the house.

"Henry told me," David said with a shrug. "You know what a gossip he is. He repeats everything he hears."

"God, he makes Mavis looked tongue-tied," Courtney snorted.

"So when do you start?" David asked.

"Start? Oh, you mean the decorating." She twisted in her seat and smiled at her brother. "Tomorrow, if we can borrow Mom's car. Joe Donelly's offered to give us a discount on the paint," she told him.

"Cool," Eric exclaimed. "What time does he open?"

"Not till eight," she said with a frown. "Oh darn, Mom's going in early tomorrow. She'll need the car."

"We're not going to let a little thing like that stop us," Eric said quickly. "We can grab a cab home."

"I can give you a lift," David volunteered. "I'm going to be out doing errands tomorrow."

Courtney remembered that Sunday was David's day off too. "Are you sure?"

"It's no problem. I'll be by at eight to pick you guys up. Maybe we can go out for breakfast afterwards or something."

Courtney fretted over David's parting remark as she got ready for bed. Was David asking her out on a date? No, he couldn't be, she thought as she rinsed her toothbrush. Eric was going to be with them. David was just being nice. He probably felt bad because they didn't have any wheels of their own.

But the next morning she dressed with extra care, putting on her good jeans and tucking a neatly tailored red blouse into the waistband. The outfit was casual, but it showed off her figure nicely.

"David's here," Eric called from downstairs.

Courtney grabbed her purse, stuffed a wad of bills she'd taken from her stash in her desk into it, and raced out.

"I hope you're not planning on painting in that outfit," Eric said with a frown.

"Of course not," she snapped. "I'll change into my grubbies when we get home."

David gave her an appreciative glance as she climbed into the front seat, but he made no comment. They chatted as they drove to the hardware store. David pulled into the parking lot and shut off the engine. "I've got to hit the grocery store and the dry cleaners," he said. "I'll meet you inside when I'm done. Okay?"

She smiled and nodded and hurried after her brother. Courtney followed Eric down the paint aisle, catching up to him in front of the semigloss enamel. "How do we know how much to buy?" she asked.

He'd already flicked out his notepad. "I measured the walls. Okay, here's the deal. You get to pick out the colors and the wallpaper, but I'm in charge of the actual work. We got a deal?"

"Deal," Courtney said quickly. "But why are you letting me do all the fun stuff?"

Eric made a face. "Come on, C.C., we both know that all my taste is in my mouth. You're good at color coordinating and stuff like that."

An hour later, Eric was probably regretting his decision. "Just pick some paint, darn it," he snapped at Courtney. "There's at least half a dozen in that bunch there that'll match the wallpaper."

"It's got to be perfect," she muttered, reaching up and snatching a pale apple-green paint sample from the top of the rack. She held the color tab next to the delicately flowered, green, pink, and white wallpaper and smiled. "This is it," she cried. "I knew if I kept looking I'd find the right color. If we trail the wallpaper from the living room into the hall, then this paint is perfect for the dining room."

"Hey, you two, ready yet?" David asked. He looked amused as he took in Courtney's sparkling eyes and Eric's dour expression.

"This should do it," she said.

"Let's hope they don't have to mix that paint," Eric muttered dangerously.

But their luck held and they found several cans

of the color they needed. At the checkout stand, Eric pulled out a wad of bills when the cashier announced the total, less the promised discount. He started to count out twenties, and then looked up in surprise when Courtney thrust several bills at him. "What's this?"

"My half," she explained. "I know you said you'd pay for it, but that's not fair."

"But you're saving your money for that ball dress or something, aren't you?" He frowned at her, not sure if he liked this new development. Not that he was all that keen to part with his own cash, but a deal was a deal and he had told Courtney he'd handle the expense of getting the supplies. Heck, he was just grateful she was going to help do the work.

She glanced to where David stood on the other side of the counter, hoping he couldn't overhear them. "I'm probably not even going to get asked to the Winter Ball, let alone need a dress. In case you haven't noticed, my social life is pretty dead. Besides, I'd like to help pay. It is Mom and Dad's Christmas present."

"Okay." Eric took the money and handed it along with his own to the cashier. "Sounds good to me. I was saving up to buy a new saw anyway."

"What kind?" the cashier asked. "We're having a sale on band saws later this month."

Eric's eyes lit up. "How much off?"

"Twenty percent," the cashier told him with a grin. "The sale starts right after Christmas—December twenty-sixth. But get here early. Those saws go pretty fast."

"Okay, that's the last one," Eric said. He pasted the last strip of paper onto the wall and then smoothed the bubbles out with a wood block.

Courtney, aching in every bone of her body, wearily stepped into the center of the room. Slowly, a huge smile spread across her face. Even with the pale light of twilight creeping in through the windows, the room looked brighter and more cheerful. As a matter of fact, it looked positively gorgeous. Even those annoying old-fashioned wall sconces looked good next to the new paper. Once she'd cleaned the things with brass polish, they shined like Christmas lights.

"I can't believe we did it," she exulted. "In one afternoon, too."

"One long, aching afternoon," Eric said as he put the wood block down next to the ladder. He came over and stood next to her. "We make a pretty good team."

"You really are good with your hands," she said.

"You're a great gofer," he replied. "And even better at following directions. Man, I'm sorry we won't have time to get the hall done before Mom and Dad get home."

"Let's see what it looks like with the lights on," he said, walking over and flicking the switch.

The living room was utterly transformed.

"This is incredible," Courtney said.

"Wait'll you see this room when we get the carpet pulled up and the panels stripped of all that grime." He glanced at his watch. "How much longer before they're home?"

"Just long enough to get things cleaned up." Courtney picked up the extra rolls of paper and headed for the closet in the hall. "Uh, Eric, we're going to do the dining room before we tackle the panels and floors, aren't we?" she asked. Much as she hated the dingy old carpet, she hated the dingy old dining room more.

"Well," Eric said slowly. "I don't know. Wouldn't it be kinda neat to get one room completely done before we move on?"

"Absolutely not," she argued, heading for the hall. "If I have to eat in that hideous room much longer, I'll become an anorexic."

"But we usually eat in the kitchen," he persisted. He picked up the ladder and followed her.

"That's because the dining room is so ugly it makes everyone lose their appetite." She yanked open the door of the large built-in closet under the stairs. "Don't try to weasel out of it. You promised we'd do the dining room next."

"Oh all right. It is pretty gross in there. Do you think the people that put up that purple paper were color-blind?"

"Nah, they just didn't have any taste," she retorted. She carefully put the rolls of paper up on the shelf. "What do you think Mom and Dad are going to say when they see what we've done?" She was a bit nervous about this. Now that it was a fait accompli, she was beginning to wonder if maybe they'd gone too far. "I mean, maybe Mom had some ideas for redecorating the house herself."

"I hope they're going to like it," he answered cautiously. "Besides, Mom was never interested in decorating. She hired someone to do our old house, remember?"

"You don't think they'll get mad at us for doing it without asking them?"

"Nah. I don't think so." Eric put the ladder into the closet and then started back to the living room for the rest of the tools. "A few months ago Mom would have probably had a hissy fit, but she's changed. So's Dad. They're both a lot less uptight than they used to be. The only thing that would freak Mom out now is if we tried to touch her flower beds."

"She wouldn't let Mel Gibson touch her flower beds," Courtney said. "And she loves him. Have you noticed how much younger they both seem these days? Dad's actually started wearing jeans and he doesn't look stupid in them, either."

"Yeah, I've noticed," Eric said thoughtfully. "Did you know they were hippies when they were in college?"

"Hippies? You mean with long hair and peace symbols and all that?" A few months ago Courtney couldn't have imagined her mother in such a way, but now the idea didn't seem all that farfetched.

Eric laughed. "The whole nine yards. When we were unpacking I went through some of their old photo albums. Dad's hair was longer than yours and Mom wore bell-bottoms and tie-dyed T-shirts. There was a picture of them at a demonstration, can you believe it?"

"You've got to be kidding. Mom and Dad demonstrating? About what?"

"Nuclear weapons," Eric replied. "I saw a Ban the Bomb sign in the background."

"I wonder if they were ever arrested?" Courtney said thoughtfully.

"Who knows? I never would have thought that Mom would love working in a nursery or that Dad would get such a charge out of clerking in a video store, but they do."

They jumped as they heard footsteps coming up

the front steps. "That's them. Quick, let's go into the living room."

Grabbing her brother's hand, Courtney dragged him into the center of the huge living room. She glanced around quickly to make sure she'd picked up all the bits and pieces of newspaper and wallpaper scraps.

"Hi, we're home," Eleanor called from the hall. "Anyone here?"

Courtney looked at Eric and nodded, giving him the chance to do the honors. "In here," he shouted. "We've got a surprise for you."

Jack and Eleanor, holding hands, stepped into the room and stopped dead. There was a moment of stunned silence. Eleanor dropped her husband's hand and came farther into the room, her eyes scanning the walls, her mouth slightly open in what Courtney hoped was pleased surprise and not stunned shock. Jack, shaking his head, followed her.

Finally Courtney couldn't stand it anymore. "Well, uh, what do you think? I hope you like it," she said, the words tumbling out in rush. "But Eric and I thought that redecorating the house would make a nice Christmas present for you . . . and . . . and . . ."

"Oh my God," Eleanor gushed, "it's beautiful." She turned, still with an expression of amazement on her face, and looked at her husband. "Isn't it gorgeous, honey? The kids did it all themselves too."

Jack grinned. "You guys did a great job." He walked over to the wall and inspected the seams. "I mean a really good job."

"Eric did all the really hard stuff," Courtney said,

her face breaking into a pleased smile. "I was just the gofer and the cleaner-upper."

"Courtney did her fair share," Eric insisted. "This present's from both of us. We're going to do the whole house."

"Are you serious?" Jack asked.

"Sure, it'll be a piece of cake." Eric grinned and glanced at his mother. "Do you really like it?"

Eleanor laughed. "I don't like it, honey"—she walked over and put her arms around her son's shoulders—"I love it. But you don't have to do the entire house. That's an enormous job."

"It's easy," he said firmly. "Especially with two of us doing it. Like C.C. said, it's going to be your Christmas present. It's going to take awhile to get it all done, though. We've only got one day a week to work."

"But we'll get it done," Courtney said as she walked over to stand next to her dad. "We're doing the dining room next."

Her father didn't say anything for a minute. He reached out and ran his hand over the paper again. "This is good wallpaper; it must have cost a lot."

"We got it at a discount," Courtney said quickly. "From Donelly's Hardware. He's one of my customers."

"I'd say this calls for a celebration," Eleanor announced. "Let's have fried chicken tonight. Eric, you and Dad go get us the biggest bucket you can find. Courtney, you and I will dig out the paper plates."

"I'll set the table." Courtney started for the kitchen.

"Bring the plates in here," Eleanor called. "I want to sit here and enjoy my new wallpaper."

Forty-five minutes later, Courtney licked her fingers and tossed a bone into the now-empty paper bucket. "That was really good."

"You ate like a pig," Eric retorted. "I thought you were going to break my arm when I reached for that last chicken leg."

"Hey, it's only fair, you got the last biscuit."

"And I have a beautiful living room," Eleanor sighed in satisfaction. "And your father has an announcement to make."

"Oh honey," Jack said, grinning sheepishly. "Don't make a big deal of it."

"It is a big deal," Eleanor said firmly.

"What is?" Courtney asked. Honestly, sometimes her parents drove her crazy. "Did Dad get a job offer?" She held her breath while she waited for his answer but her hope died when he shook his head.

"No, honey, I got asked to speak at the library. It seems the librarian is a friend of Harry Reardon's, the *Gazette* publisher. I guess he mentioned that I was doing a column for the paper and said that I was some kind of local expert on films. She dropped by the video store, talked to me for a while, and then asked if I'd come speak to a senior citizens group that meets there." Jack shrugged, trying to look casual. "I told her I'd think about it and let her know."

Courtney stared at her father for a moment. He was really getting into this film thing. But despite his casual manner, despite his attempts to make it sound like it wasn't important, she could tell that it was. That it made him feel good about himself. "What is there to think about? You'd be terrific."

"Thanks, sweetheart," he said, "but I've never done a lot of public speaking. Maybe I wouldn't be any good at it."

"Sure you have," Eric chimed in. "You were always giving seminars and training speeches when you worked at TechniQuik."

"But that was different," Jack argued. "I knew what I was talking about."

"You'll know what you're talking about now too," Courtney persisted. "You know more about movies than anyone I know. Come on, Dad, admit it. You've seen every B movie, every sci-fi and horror film, every murder mystery ever made," she broke off to take a breath and wondered why she was encouraging him. She should be urging him to keep sending his résumés out.

"You've seen all those foreign films too," Eleanor added. "I ought to know—you've made me sit through enough of those boring turkeys."

"How can you say they were boring?" Jack exclaimed.

Eleanor waved her hand impatiently. "That's not the point. You'll be great at this and you know it. Why shouldn't you share your expertise with other people? They're interested or the library wouldn't have asked."

"Come on, Dad," Courtney said. "Do it. I'll come and hear you. I'll invite Allison and Jackie too, it'll be cool."

Jack laughed. "Okay, okay, you've talked me into it."

"Take your poster collection," Eric said excitedly. "That'd really be neat." Their father had an extensive collection of movie posters.

"That's a good idea. I've picked up some really good ones lately from the store too." He relaxed back against the cushions. "One of the fringe benefits of my job."

Eleanor got up and started clearing up the paper plates. Eric rose, stretched, and yawned. "I think I'll hit the sack. I'm beat."

As soon as Courtney and her father were alone, she turned to him. "You really like this job, don't you?" she asked softly. One part of her didn't want to hear the answer, but another part of her did.

Jack looked at her thoughtfully. "Well, it doesn't pay very well and I'm on my feet most of the day. But, I do get to talk about movies and see all the latest releases. So, yes, I guess I do like it. Why? Does it bother you that your old man doesn't mind being a clerk?"

She shook her head. "No, work is work. I just wondered if you liked this job so much that you'd stopped looking for a job like the one you had at TechniQuik."

Before he could answer her, there was a knock on the front door. "I'll get it," Eric yelled.

Curious, Courtney turned to see who was dropping by unannounced. When she saw the tall figure walking in behind her brother, her jaw dropped. It was David.

"Hey, look who's here," Eric said. "It's David, Courtney's boss."

Jack rose to his feet, his expression curious. "How do you do," he said. "I'm Jack Cutler. Courtney's father."

"I hope you don't mind my dropping in," David said, flashing a smile at Courtney. "But I gave Courtney and Eric a lift to the hardware store this morning and as I was in the neighborhood I thought I'd stop by and see how the room turned out."

"See for yourself," Courtney said proudly. But

David was already scanning the newly papered walls.

"You two do good work," he said. "Do you hire out?"

"Not for what you pay," Courtney shot back.

Everyone laughed. They exchanged pleasantries for a few more minutes and then Jack and Eric excused themselves.

Courtney was at a loss. "Uh, would you like some coffee?" she asked David.

"Yeah, that's the other reason I came by."

She blinked.

"If you're not busy or too tired," he continued quickly, "I thought we could go to a coffeehouse I know near the college and, well, have coffee."

CHAPTER
EIGHT

December 14th

Dear Diary,

David is right downstairs! He dropped by to see the decorating. I'm snatching a few minutes to write in you because my nerd-boy brother dragged David out to look at his wood shop. I'm so excited I had to do something. Never in my wildest dreams did I ever think I'd be going out for coffee with David. But I am. I don't know if this is a date or not?????? But, geez, I hope so. I'll write more later.

David took her to a small coffeehouse near Landsdale Junior College. Courtney tried not to stare when she stepped inside and followed David to one of the small, wooden tables in the huge, crowded room.

"What'll you have?" he asked.

She gazed at him blankly. "Uh, coffee, I guess. This is a coffeehouse, right?"

"There's lots of different kinds here," he told her, laughing. "You want me to pick something for you?"

She smiled gratefully. "Just make sure it's something that won't take the roof off my mouth."

"Leave it to me," he said, heading for the counter.

Courtney took a deep breath, inhaling the rich, pungent odors of the exotic scents filling the air. She leaned back and took a moment to examine her surroundings.

David had told her the place had once been a small warehouse. The walls were brick and the concrete floor was painted a bright, fire-engine red. Woven rush mats and rag rugs placed in strategic areas gave the place an air of homeyness. Bookcases, some holding magazines, some with books in them, were placed willy-nilly around the walls. A long counter with clear glass bins full of coffee beans bisected the room and from two huge speakers mounted on the wall, the low, soothing strains of classical music filled the air.

"I hope you like this blend," David put a cup in front of her. "It's a Kona, real smooth and not too bitter."

"I'm sure it'll be fine." She picked up the colorful mug, took a sip, and smiled. "It's good."

"It's one of my favorites." David sat down opposite her and leaned back in his chair. "This time of night my stomach can't handle anything really strong."

Courtney suddenly felt tongue-tied. David was apparently at ease, the atmosphere was just perfect, and she couldn't think of a blessed thing to say. "Do you come here often?" she finally asked.

"I don't have a lot of free time, but I drop in whenever I can. It's a popular place with the college crowd."

"I can see why," she murmured, picking up her coffee and taking another sip to give her hands something to do. "The atmosphere is really nice."

"Yeah, the atmosphere's good," he agreed, "and as it's Landsdale's only coffeehouse, it doesn't have a lot of competition." He grinned. "They do a lot of poetry readings and that kind of stuff here. But that's not the reason we come."

"Why, then?" She laughed and started to relax.

"Because coming here and pouring exotically fla-vored coffee down our throats makes us all feel cool and sophisticated. Besides, the coffee's actually good. A lot better than the Victorian Café."

"Hey," she protested, "I like our coffee."

"That's because you don't know any better," he charged. "You only had your first cup a few months ago. I know, I was watching you the first time you drank it."

She cringed, remembering how Mavis and Joe and some of the other regulars had coaxed her into drinking that first cup and then laughed their heads off as she'd added six creamers of half-and-half. "No fair. That one was from the bottom of the pot. My coffee's really good these days. Good enough to get a discount from Joe Donelly at the hardware store."

"Donelly gives everyone a discount," he teased. "He even gave Lannie one and she made lousy cof-fee."

She made a face at him, which only made him laugh again.

"So, what are you doing for entertainment these days?" he asked casually.

"Hanging wallpaper," Courtney snorted deli-cately. "Between working and school and studying, I don't have time to do much of anything. Now that I've let Eric talk me into redoing the house as Mom and Dad's Christmas present, I'll have even less time."

"It'll be worth it though," he said. "That living room looks great. Maybe things will ease up a little next year? Are you going to Landsdale JC?"

Courtney thought for a moment. "Probably. Unless my parents were to win the lottery, they're not going to have the cash to send me to Prior." Strangely enough, knowing her dream of going away to college was as dead as yesterday's news didn't depress her as much as she'd thought it might. Living in San Francisco and going to Prior would have been fun, but she'd learned that when one dream died, life sometimes gave you another. At least she hoped that was the case.

"That's the women's college in San Francisco, right?"

She nodded. "A friend and I had planned on going together. But that was before my dad lost his job."

"Things change, huh?"

"And not always for the better," she agreed. "What about you? Still planning on going to UCSD?" She crossed her fingers under the table and then quickly uncrossed them. Just because she had a crush on David she certainly shouldn't hope that his dream went up in smoke. But she hated the idea of him moving all the way to San Diego.

He studied her for a moment and then shrugged. "Actually, I think I'm going to be staying right here."

"But I thought you wanted to be a marine biologist," she exclaimed.

"I still do," he said firmly. "But it looks like I've got a shot at a full scholarship to UC Santa Barbara."

"Wow, a full scholarship," she replied, impressed. "No one in their right mind would pass that up."

"You got that right," he said, nodding. "If I go to San Diego, I'll have to take out a student loan. That's a real drag. It would mean that when I finally did graduate, I'd be saddled with debt up to my ears. If I take the Santa Barbara scholarship, I could keep on living at home," he explained, "until I get my undergraduate degree. With a scholarship, I could save quite a wad of cash and then take my advanced degree without having to work my tail off to keep a roof over my head. If I get good enough grades, I could probably go to UCSD for grad school. You need at least a master's degree and preferably a Ph.D. to get anywhere as a marine biologist."

"You'll do good enough," she said firmly. "You work harder than anyone I've ever seen."

David smiled self-consciously. "You work pretty hard yourself. What about you? What's your dream?"

She thought about it for a moment. The only dream she really had was to get her old life back. But she wasn't going to admit that to him. She shrugged nonchalantly. "Right now, I'm just concentrating on earning enough tip money to buy a class ring."

"That shouldn't be a problem." He leaned forward on his elbow. "You've become a much better waitress."

"And my tips have risen accordingly," she teased. "As for wanting anything else, I guess I just want to hang on long enough to save up enough cash for a used car and maybe a new dress if I get asked to the Winter Ball—" She broke off and clamped her mouth shut. Damn. Now he'd think she was hinting for a date.

"You'll need a car when you go to college," he said thoughtfully. "Some of your classes might be at night. With all the cutbacks in funding, you've got to grab a class when it's offered."

"Yeah," she relaxed. "That's what I was thinking. I've been putting my salary in the bank. But it's probably going to take a long time to save up enough even for an old heap."

"You know anything about cars?"

"No."

"Does Eric or your dad?" he asked seriously.

"Not really. Eric's good with his hands but I don't think he knows a heck of a lot about the internal combustion engine. Dad's all thumbs with everything."

"Then you're one lucky girl." He leaned toward her and smiled broadly. "I do happen to know about cars. When you've got a wad saved up, I'll go with you and keep you from getting a lemon."

Courtney fell into bed with a smile on her face. David had volunteered to take her car hunting. That must mean, she thought as she pulled the covers up to her chin, that he thought of her as more than just a coworker. *But does it?* She couldn't quite get a handle on their relationship. When he'd driven her home, he'd turned to her in the car. The atmosphere had reeked of intimacy. The low strains of soft rock coming from the radio, the warm coziness of the front seat, and the way they sat close together on the bench seat, their legs almost but not quite touching. She'd been sure he was going to kiss her.

But all he'd done was reach across and undo her seat belt.

Courtney cringed inwardly as she recalled that awkward moment. She'd leaned toward him, her face close to his. He'd smiled and said, "Thanks for coming out for coffee. I'll see you at work tomorrow."

There'd been nothing to do but grab the door handle and scramble out with as much dignity as she could muster. But he'd said he'd take her car hunting; she hugged that thought to her as she closed her eyes. That must mean something.

But apparently it didn't mean a darned thing. Because the next day at work, David was once again the boss and she was just one of his employees. She shoved a rack of glasses onto the top of the back counter and then reached for the coffeepot. As she turned to refill cups, she glanced up as the front door opened.

"Allison." Courtney smiled in delight. "What are you doing here?"

Allison gave her a wan smile and sat down on a stool at the counter. "Just thought I'd pop over and see you, that's all. Can I have a Coke?"

Courtney peered at her friend closely. Allison's eyes were red and slightly puffy, like she'd been crying.

"Tell you what," Courtney said brightly, "I get off in a few minutes—"

"Good, I'll give you a lift home," Allison interrupted. "Cancel the Coke, then. Uh, do you have plans for the evening?"

"Just my English homework," Courtney replied. "But it's only reading and I can do it tomorrow morning. Why?"

"I thought maybe we could grab a bite of dinner

somewhere," Allison said casually. "You haven't eaten, have you?"

"No." Courtney was so sick of hamburgers and fried food that she'd stopped eating a meal during her break. She usually just had something to drink and then grabbed a yogurt or a sandwich at home. "Tell you what, we can go to that new taco joint over on Main. Okay?"

"Yeah, that sounds okay."

Something was wrong, very wrong. Courtney could tell that Allison needed to talk to her. She quickly finished cleaning the coffee urn, wiped her hands, and then dashed back to the time clock and punched out.

But Allison didn't say anything about what was wrong as she drove across town. She just stared straight ahead, answering only when spoken to and then in words of one syllable. Courtney feared the worst.

But she waited until after they were seated in a cheerful orange booth in the back of the Spicy Tamale before demanding an answer.

"Okay, what gives?" she asked as soon as the waitress had taken their order. "What's got you so upset?"

Allison's eyes filled with tears and her lips trembled. "Oh God, Court, it's awful. Just awful."

"Are you pregnant?" Courtney asked softly. Allison and Jared Pronsky had been pretty hot and heavy lately.

Allison laughed harshly. "Don't be silly, I'm not that dumb. It's my dad."

Courtney's heart sank. *Darn. Allison's dad must be having an affair.* "Oh no. Is he seeing another woman? Is that why he's been dying his hair and working out?"

Allison shook her head and brushed an escaping tear off her cheek. "He's lost his job!"

"Lost his job?" Courtney echoed, relieved. "Is that all?"

"Is that all?" Allison's mouth gaped open in shock. "What the hell do you mean? Don't you understand? We have no money, no savings, no nothing. Not only is Dad losing his job, but he announced that it's taken every cent he's earned the past few years just to pay the bills. There's nothing in reserve, no savings account, no stocks and bonds, nothing."

"That's typical," Courtney muttered. "With the cost of living, it's tough for anyone to save these days."

"Don't you get it?" Allison continued as though Courtney hadn't spoken. "We're ruined. We can't even make the house or the car payments next month. I won't be able to go to Prior, I won't be able to do anything. This is serious. For crying out loud, it's a calamity."

"It's a pain in the butt," Courtney said calmly, "but no one's dying and you're not in the streets starving."

"We will be if he doesn't find another one pretty darned quick," Allison snapped. Her face crumpled and she quickly ducked her head.

"I'm sorry," Courtney apologized hastily. She reached across the table and put her hand over Allison's. "I know how you feel, I know what you're going through. I've been there, remember?"

Tears falling freely, Allison looked up. "Then why are you being so mean?"

"I wasn't trying to be mean." Courtney felt like a worm. "I was trying to be casual."

A small sob escaped and Allison ducked her head again.

"Believe it or not," Courtney continued softly, "it's not the end of the world. You will survive. Your father will find another job."

Allison snorted. "He doesn't seem to think so. He's known for months he might be laid off and he didn't say a word, not one damned word. His company is doing something called restructuring. That's why he was working out and dying his hair and dressing so much younger. He knew he might have to start job hunting and he said his odds for finding something else would be better the younger he looked." She shook her head. "But darn it, that's not fair. Isn't age discrimination against the law?"

Courtney grinned as she looked at Allison's outraged expression. At least the waterworks had stopped. "Of course it is, but it happens anyway. But stop worrying, he'll find another job."

"Like your father did?" Allison snorted again. "How long's it been now? Six months?"

"Four," Courtney corrected.

"Whatever, four or six," Allison waved dismissively. "Does he have job offers pouring in?"

"Well, not yet," Courtney mumbled, not sure if she liked what Allison was getting at. "But he will. These things take time. Good jobs don't grow on trees, you know. Lots of companies are downsizing and laying people off. But he'll find something eventually."

"That's what I mean," Allison pointed out. "If it's taken your dad this long, it might take mine just as long."

"It might," Courtney agreed. She thought of her own father. He was still sending out résumés and following up leads. Yet these days, he seemed to be doing it more out of habit than anything else. His attitude secretly worried her. Despite her bravado in front of Allison, Courtney did want her own father to have a good job again. It would sure make life easier.

"I can't believe you're being so casual about this," Allison charged. "You were the one person who I thought would understand."

"I do understand," Courtney protested. "That's why I know it's not as bad as it seems right now. You've had a nasty shock, Allison, but it's not the end of the world." But she remembered all too well how'd she'd felt when it had happened to her family. It had meant the end of world she'd been used to living in, but she didn't think this was the best time to point that out to Allison. They'd survived. Heck, they'd more than survived.

"But it might take him months to find a job with a comparable salary," Allison argued. "What do we do in the meantime? Starve? Go homeless?"

"You do what everyone else does," Courtney said bluntly. Shocked or not, she wasn't doing Allison any favors by mincing words. The sooner she faced the fact that her life had changed, the faster she could get off her butt and do something about it. "Get a job. Your mom can work too. My mom does. Frankly, it's been the best thing that ever happened to her. She's a lot less cranky and uptight than she used to be. Besides, working isn't all that bad. I've made a lot of new friends. Having money I've actually earned is kind of neat—"

"But I don't want to make any new friends," Allison wailed. "I liked my life just the way it was. I don't want to get a job. This is my senior year, for God's sake. I want to have fun. I want to enjoy myself and be a kid."

"Sometimes," Courtney said softly, "we don't get what we want in life."

"But it's not fair."

"Who said life was fair?" Courtney shot back. Then she caught herself. Allison's words sounded like a playback of herself from four months ago. She sighed. Right now, Allison needed comfort and reassurance, not a speech to keep her chin up. "But you'll find that things aren't as miserable as they seem. Really, you'll do just fine."

Allison started to cry again. "What if we lose our home and have to move?"

"That's not going to happen." But even to Courtney's own ears, the words sounded hollow.

Allison swiped at a tear and hiccuped softly. "It happened to you."

"Having to sell our house hurt," Courtney said honestly. "But it didn't kill me."

"But I love my house," Allison sniffed. "I can't remember living anywhere else."

"You probably won't have to, either." Courtney reached over and patted her hand again. "And even if you do, there's some neat things about moving. For starters, it's interesting moving to a different neighborhood." She was surprised that she actually meant what she was saying. "Our neighbors now are real different from the people in the Estates."

"But I don't like things that are different," Allison said softly. "It scares me."

"It scared me too," Courtney admitted. "But it's not all bad. When we lived at our other house, we

never even spoke to our neighbors. Everyone was
too busy working to earn enough money to pay
those big mortgages to have time to visit. But now,
in the new house, we've already gotten to know the
two old guys that live next door and Mrs. Bassett,
the widow who lives across the street, and lots of
other people."

"Are they nice?"

"Some of them are nice," Courtney said, "and
some of them are creeps. But the point is, we know
them. When Mrs. Bassett goes away to spend the
weekend with her daughter in San Diego, everyone
in the neighborhood keeps an eye on her place. It's
not the same, Allison, but it's not bad either. And
the two old guys next door, the Parfait twins, they
fight all the time"—she laughed remembering last
week's spat—"and every time they have a tiff, Harold—he's the oldest one—he stomps off in a huff
and won't come home until Oscar puts a white flag
in the front window."

Even Allison laughed. "You've got to be kidding."

"No. Last week Harold slept under Mrs. Bassett's
roses for three days before Oscar put the flag up. It
was touch and go there for a few days; Mrs. Bassett
was getting so teed off with finding Harold in her
front yard every morning, she threatened to use the
water hose."

For the rest of the week, Courtney made it a point
to call Allison every evening when she got home
from work. By Sunday night, Allison had calmed
down a little and wasn't so scared about the future.

Courtney put the phone down and glanced down
the hall toward the kitchen. Eric and her parents
were behind the closed door, probably digging into

the submarine sandwiches her brother had brought home for everyone's supper tonight.

She yawned, debating whether to go and eat or just head straight upstairs to the shower. But her stomach rumbled, so she kicked off her shoes and wandered in the direction of food. Pushing the door open, she stepped inside.

Courtney paused. Eric and her parents were sitting around the table. But the sandwiches were still in the brown paper bag, no one had gotten sodas out of the fridge, and everyone's expression was deadly serious. Her stomach plummeted. It had to be something awful to stop her brother from stuffing his face. "What's wrong?"

Eleanor gave her a weak smile. "Nothing's wrong, honey. But I'm glad you're here. We're having a family council."

"About what?" Courtney said suspiciously. The last time they'd all looked this serious her father had lost his job. "Has someone gotten fired?"

"No," Jack said with a grin. "Just the opposite. Come on, sit down and let's eat. We've got a lot to talk about."

Courtney sat down at her usual place. Eleanor reached for the bag and began unloading sandwiches.

"I'll get the sodas and the paper plates," Eric said, getting up and going to the fridge. As soon as he was directly behind Jack, he jerked his head toward the hall, indicating he wanted to talk to Courtney privately.

"No secrets, now," Eleanor said quickly. She'd spotted Eric's head jerking. "I don't want you prejudicing your sister. This decision involves everyone."

Eric frowned but said nothing.

He brought back a six-pack of cola and a stack of paper plates and dumped them in the center of the table.

"What's this all about?" Courtney asked curiously. She wasn't scared anymore. She didn't know if it was because she was getting used to life throwing her curveballs or whether it was because the others seemed preoccupied and not worried. But whatever the case, she decided not to have hysterics until she heard what was going on.

"Let's eat first," Eleanor said firmly. "We'll all think better on a full stomach." She passed out the sandwiches and then opened a carton of cole slaw.

"I like using paper plates," Eric said around a mouthful of food. "It sure beats doing dishes."

"I like it too," Eleanor agreed. "But it's hell on the environment. All those trees being chopped down."

They finished their meal quickly and cleaned up. When they were all seated again, Jack cleared his throat. "I've got two announcements to make," he began. "First of all, John Cleary, the owner of Wildheart Videos, is opening another branch at that new strip mall on Edgars Street. He's going to be running that store and he's asked me to take over as manager of my store."

"That's great, Dad," Courtney said, genuinely proud of her father. "Will you get a raise?"

Jack chuckled. "Quite a nice one," he said, "but even with the raise, I won't come anywhere close to matching my old salary."

"That's okay," Eric said quickly. "We're doing okay. I mean, so what if we don't have a lot of cash—"

"Eric," Eleanor said in a warning tone. "Let your dad finish."

Courtney glanced at their faces, puzzled by everyone's attitude.

"Sorry, Dad," Eric mumbled. He shot Courtney a quick look, his eyes narrowed as though he was silently trying to send her a message.

"It's okay, son," Jack said. "Anyway, like I was saying. Even with a raise, working as a manager of a video store won't come close to bringing in what I used to make. That's one thing I want to make perfectly clear." He looked directly at Courtney.

"And . . . ?" she prompted. Why was everyone acting so weird?

"And, well, the point is, I've been offered another job."

"From another video chain?" Courtney guessed. She'd heard that one of the big chains was building a store over on the other side of the mall.

"No, not from another video chain." He took a deep breath, almost as though he were bracing himself, and said, "I've been offered a job by Tarleton Computers."

Courtney couldn't believe it. "You mean a good job, like the one you had at TechniQuik?"

"He's got a good job at the video store," Eric snapped.

"Eric," Eleanor warned. "We already know how you feel. Now we want to find out how Courtney feels."

"Very much like the one I had at TechniQuik, only I'd earn a little less. I'd be a department head instead of a division manager. So what do you think, honey?" Her father gave her a warm smile. "Tarleton's offering a full benefits and pension plan package. What do you think I should do?"

Were they all crazy? Courtney couldn't believe this. Were they actually discussing whether her father should take a high-paying job at a major company, with benefits and insurance and all that good stuff, or keep on managing a video store? Had they lost their minds? And why were they asking her opinion anyway? "Why are we discussing it?"

"Because the decision will affect you," Jack said.

"From now on, we discuss everything that affects us all," Eleanor added. "Remember, it's not just your dad's life we're talking about. We live together and what one does affects us all. Dad would have to commute down to Thousand Oaks again and he'd also have to put in some long, hard hours."

"But he used to do that at TechniQuik," Courtney pointed out. She was confused. Terribly, terribly confused. Though no one had said anything, she had the feeling that no one else but her wanted her father to take the job. But that was crazy. Did they like being poor?

"Yeah, and he hated it," Eric exclaimed. "We never saw him. He was always at work or if he wasn't physically at work, he was on the phone or too tired to do anything but sit and stare at the idiot box."

Courtney didn't want to hear any more. She wanted a class ring, she wanted to cut back on her hours at work, she wanted a new dress for the Winter Ball. For God's sake, she wanted a normal, happy senior year. Was that too much to ask?

"Well, honey," her father prompted, "what do you think?"

Courtney looked down at the table; she didn't want to meet her brother's eyes. "Well, you're not getting any younger and the job at Tarleton's does have a pension. That's something to think about."

"Yes, it is," her father said patiently. "But all that aside, what do you think I should do? Your mother and brother both seem to think we're better off as a family if I stay on at Wildheart."

"Gee, Dad," Courtney said. "Shouldn't the decision be up to you?"

"I will make the decision," he said, "but I want to know what everyone thinks. Go on, spit it out now. Give me your opinion."

Courtney took a deep breath. "I think you ought to take the job."

CHAPTER
NINE

December 22nd

Dear Diary,
  I don't believe this. Last night Dad announced he's been offered a new job and the rest of the family doesn't think he ought to accept it! Are they crazy or what? After we had the family council meeting, everyone kind of treated me like I was some sort of worm or something just because I told Dad he ought to take the new job. I mean, what did I do wrong? Eric wouldn't even look at me and I could tell by Mom's face that she was disappointed with my opinion.

Courtney sighed, closed her diary, and shoved it in the drawer. She only had a few minutes before she had to leave for the bus stop and work. Darn, it had been a lousy day all around. She'd felt so crummy she hadn't been able to concentrate in class, she'd completely forgotten she was supposed to meet Jackie at the library at lunch, and then, to top it off, she'd lost a five-dollar bill. It had been the last day of school before Christmas break, too. A day she'd normally have enjoyed because it meant that for the next two weeks she wouldn't have to drag herself out of bed at the crack of dawn.

There was a knock on Courtney's bedroom door. "It's open," she called, thinking it was her brother.

But it was her mother who stepped inside. "Hi. What time do you have to leave for work?"

"In about ten minutes," Courtney replied. "But I've got to change first."

"Good, then we have a few minutes to talk." Eleanor flopped down on the foot of the bed. "Go right ahead and change, honey. It won't bother me."

Courtney went to her closet and pulled out a navy blue A-line skirt and a white T-shirt. "What's up?" she asked.

Eleanor cleared her throat. "I wanted to talk to you about last night."

"Last night? You mean the family meeting?" Courtney pulled off her jeans and tossed them onto her dirty clothes pile at the back of her closet. "You mean the fact that you and Eric looked at me like I was the Wicked Witch of the West just because I'm sick of being poor?"

Eleanor sighed. "Oh, honey, I'm sorry. I didn't mean for it to come off like that. I just want you to understand what it will mean if your dad takes that job."

"It'll mean we don't have to scrimp and save and watch every darned penny," Courtney said as she slipped on her skirt.

Eleanor didn't say anything for a moment and Courtney glanced over her shoulder. Her mother was staring out the window, her expression thoughtful.

"Well, aren't I right?" Courtney prompted. "It'll

mean we won't be poor anymore, right?"

"Maybe," Eleanor replied slowly. "But has it really been that bad?"

Courtney shrugged. It really hadn't been that awful. But she didn't want to admit it. "It hasn't been any picnic."

"No, it hasn't been a picnic, but it hasn't been punishment park either," Eleanor said firmly. "There's a few facts you don't understand, honey."

Courtney reached for her shirt. "Like what?"

"Like the fact that this new job might not last very long," she said. "The world has changed. Just because your father has been offered a good job doesn't mean the company won't turn around and lay him off the minute the economy dims."

"But why would they hire him in the first place if they were just going to lay him off?"

Eleanor shrugged. "Because for the moment they need someone with his skills. But the minute someone says 'downsizing' or the top brass figures out the shareholders will make a big profit by cutting costs, then he could be out the door. It happens all the time. All you have to do is read the paper and you see hundreds of people getting laid off at companies that are making huge profits."

"That's lousy," Courtney muttered.

"Lousy or not, that's the way the world is these days," Eleanor continued. "There's a few other things you ought to know. If he does take the job, your father will have to commute every day. He'll be working sixty hours a week, popping antacids, and generally being as stressed out as he used to be."

Courtney bit her lip. As much as she only wanted to remember the up side of their old life, there had been a down side too. When her dad had been home, he'd been so tired and cranky that all he ever did was sleep or watch videos. There hadn't been any family sessions sharing pizza around the kitchen table, or discussing movies or books or their crazy customers. But darn it, she was tired of being poor. Didn't she have a right to expect a decent life? "Lots of people work long hours. Do you like having to work so hard?" she challenged.

Eleanor laughed. "If you're asking will I quit my job if Dad takes this one, the answer's no. I like working, I like interacting with people, even the bitchy ones. Most of all, I like being able to help people create beautiful environments with natural things. So even if Dad made a million dollars a year, I'd keep right on doing my job. Besides, even if he takes the new job, we wouldn't go back to our old spending habits. The one committment your dad and I have made is that no matter what it takes, we'll never go into debt again. From now on, we'll live within our means."

"Okay," Courtney said. "So you like your job. Does Eric like his? Do I like mine? . . ."

"I don't know, do you?" Eleanor asked.

Courtney picked up her work shoes and plopped down on the bed. She wasn't sure she wanted to answer this question but she could feel her mother watching her. "It hasn't been that bad," she finally muttered, ducking her head to avoid meeting her mother's eyes. The truth was, she did like her job. Waiting tables wasn't always fun. But she liked most of the customers and the people she worked with. Especially one particular person.

"Would you quit if Dad takes this job?" Eleanor persisted.

Courtney jerked her head up. She opened her mouth, but she couldn't think of what to say. She honestly didn't know if she would stop working. One part of her relished the pride and the independence that earning a paycheck gave her. She thought about how she'd felt when she and Eric had taken on the task of redecorating the house. Despite the hard work and her aching back, she remembered how she'd felt when they'd finished. Darn, this was a tough one.

"I'm not sure," she mumbled. "Look, it's getting late. I've got to get to work. Besides, Dad will do what he wants. My opinion doesn't count for all that much."

Eleanor stood up too and the two of them headed for the stairs. "But your opinion does count, honey," Eleanor said gently as Courtney reached the bottom. "Your dad feels very guilty because of the way your life had to change so suddenly. He hated seeing you drop out of the cheerleading squad and he hated not being able to give you a car and a clothing allowance. Believe me, he's agonizing over this choice."

"You think I ought to tell him that it doesn't matter to me what he does?" Courtney said. "You think it would be better for him if I told him to turn the job down and go on like we are?"

"I think," her mother said softly, "that it would be better for all of us."

It started to rain as she got off the bus. Courtney ran for the front door of the Victorian Café. As she stepped inside, she stopped briefly, inhaling the hot, greasy odor of sizzling burgers and fries.

"Hi," Henry yelled from behind the high counter

that separated the kitchen from the counter. "Have you heard the news?"

"What news?" She started toward the back.

"David's quitting."

She stopped in her tracks. "Quitting? Are you sure?" Geez, could the day get any worse?

"Ask him yourself," Henry said, jerking his head toward the office. "He wants to talk to you."

Courtney hurried to the time clock and punched in. Then she dashed to the office. David was sitting behind the desk, a cup of coffee in one hand and a pen in the other. He was tapping the pen against a sheaf of invoices. "Hi," Courtney said softly. "I hear you're leaving."

"Good old Henry," David said, laughing. "I see he didn't even let you clock in before he told you."

"So it's true?" She desperately hoped it wasn't. The idea of not seeing him almost every day filled her with dread.

"Yeah," he said softly. He nodded at the chair across from the desk. "Have a seat."

"Shouldn't I get out on the floor?" She cast a worried glance toward the restaurant. She wasn't sure she wanted to hear this anyway.

"Amy can cover it," he said. "Come on, I really do want to talk to you about this."

"Why?" she asked as she sat down. "It's none of my business."

"Get off it, Courtney," he scoffed, "of course it's your business. I hope I'm a little more to you than just a boss."

She wasn't sure she understood what he meant but she was so shaken by all the crazy developments in her life that she didn't trust herself to say anything except "Okay."

"I got offered a job at the college."

"Landsdale JC?"

He nodded. "Managing the cafeteria. Looks like all the years I've put in here have paid off. The pay is great, a third more than I'm making here. Even better, I'll be right on campus for both my job and my classes so that'll give me more free time. I've got one more semester there. But I'll hang onto the job even after transferring to UCSB. With the increase in salary, I should be able to save up for graduate school."

"When do you leave?"

"My replacement should be here next week. Saturday will be my last day." He smiled. "Don't look so down, they're sending Tom Parks over to manage this place. He's a nice old guy—you'll like him."

She got up. "Yes, I'm sure he'll be fine." Her heart was breaking but no way was she going to let it show. David was treating her like a friend and an employee. Breaking the news gently because he probably knew she had a crush on him. "I'd better get out to the floor now. Thanks for telling me."

She dashed out to the hall, grateful that the lighting was dim so no one could see the tears welling up in her eyes. Blinking hard, she took a deep breath and got herself under control. She was darned if she'd let anyone see how miserable she was. But heck, she really liked David. More than she'd ever liked anyone. Now he was walking out of her life. *Damn.*

Courtney busied herself cleaning coffeepots, refilling creamer baskets, and waiting on her customers. If she was a little less than cheerful, none of the regulars seemed to notice. Right before she was due to get off, Allison walked in and took a seat at the counter.

"Hi," Allison smiled broadly. "Can I have a Coke, please."

The last thing Courtney wanted to do was talk to her best friend. But then she realized that she was being selfish. Allison had a few problems of her own. "Sure. How's it going?"

Allison shrugged. "Okay. Mom's job hunting now." She snorted. "I've no idea what she thinks she can do."

"Probably lots of things," Courtney replied, putting the Coke in front of her friend. "At least she's looking."

"I'm looking too," Allison yelped. "So's Dad. But so far, no luck."

"You'll find something," Courtney replied. "It just takes awhile."

"I've put in applications at the Spicy Tamale and that boutique over on Central," Allison said. "But no one's called me in for an interview."

"Go for the Spicy Tamale," Courtney said quickly. "The boutique won't pay much more than minimum wage. At least as a waitress you'll get tips. They really add up."

Allison took a sip of her Coke and sighed. "Job hunting is really the pits. Especially when you don't have any experience. How am I supposed to get experience if no one will give me a chance?"

Courtney nodded sympathetically. "You have to keep on trying. No matter how discouraged you get, you just keep on putting in applications, and eventually you'll run across someone who's desperate for help and is willing to give you a chance. That's how I got my job."

Allison laughed. "They have to be desperate? Why? Am I that unemployable?"

Courtney was relieved that her friend was finding her sense of humor again. "No, but you are inexperienced. Don't worry, so was I. But I found a job. You will too. Just don't give up." A wave of guilt washed over her as she heard herself playing cheerleader for Allison. Who was she kidding? Here she was giving Allison advice when she herself was hoping that her father would have a good job soon and she wouldn't be so poor. She felt like the worst kind of hypocrite.

"I don't have much choice in the matter," Allison admitted honestly. "We need money. I can't believe this is happening. Who'd have thought that people like you and me would be in this kind of a spot? Just last summer we were two carefree high school girls. The biggest worry we had was whether or not we'd make cheerleader. Now I'm worried about how we're going to make the mortgage payment." She made a face. "Oh hell, don't get me started."

"I know how you feel, Allison," Courtney said. "I felt the same way myself. It's not fair. But then again, whoever said life had to be?"

"Yeah, I guess you're right. Anyway, how about a ride home?" Allison grinned. "You'd better say yes pretty quick, too—I may not have my car much longer."

"You have to sell your car?"

"Only if I don't find a job by February. My folks can't make the insurance payments anymore. It's free and clear so we don't have to worry about finance payments. But if I'm not gainfully employed by the time the next premium is due, I'll have to sell it."

Courtney finished up and went to clock out. As she was heading down the hall, David stuck his head out of the office. "Courtney, hang on a minute."

She stopped, turned, and looked at him expectantly.

"Uh, being as Saturday's my last day, I was wondering if you'd like to go out with me Saturday night."

She couldn't believe it. He was asking her for a date. A real date. Her depression lifted like a balloon in a high wind. She gave him a wide smile. "Sure, but I don't get off until ten."

He laughed. "I know. Maybe we can have a late dinner and then go over to the coffeehouse and talk. Does that sound good?"

It sounded like heaven.

Courtney was in such a good mood that she treated herself to a nice, soothing bubble bath. Closing her eyes, she relaxed against the back of the tub. What a day this had been! She couldn't get her mother's words out of her mind. Did her dad hate the idea of going back to work in a high-level management job? Was she the only one who was tired of being poor? *Has it been so bad?*

She shifted in the tub, opened her eyes, and stared at the ceiling. This room hadn't been redone yet and she could see the fine lines of old, cracked paint directly over her head. Maybe they could do this room next. Maybe they could hire someone to redo it if her father had a good job. . . . Strangely enough, the idea didn't have as much appeal as she'd thought it might. She liked redecorating. She thought of how she and Eric had redone the living room. Radio blaring, chugging cans of soft drink, they'd wallpapered until their arms ached. But the results had been worth it. The room looked beautiful and they'd done it themselves. Both her parents had been real impressed. She'd heard her mom on the phone to one of her friends, bragging about what great kids she had.

But Courtney didn't feel so great now. Her mother and brother didn't want her dad to take the job. They liked their life now. But darn it, she thought, they didn't have to go without a class ring and senior pictures.

She sighed, pulled the plug out, and stood up. Reaching for a towel, she saw her hazy reflection in the steamed mirror. That was how she felt now. Hazy. Like she didn't know what she wanted and if she made the wrong move, everything would fall apart again.

"Hey, Courtney," Eric banged on the door. "Get a move on, I want to talk to you."

She rolled her eyes. "Give me a minute." Darn, she hoped she wasn't in for another lecture from her brother. She'd had about all she could take today.

But when she opened the door, he was still standing there. She could tell by the look on his face that she wasn't going to be going to sleep anytime soon. "Look," she began, "before you lay into me, I want you to know that I'm not being a totally selfish bitch about this thing."

Eric blinked in surprise. "I never thought you were. Let's go to my room to talk, okay? I don't want Mom or Dad overhearing us."

She followed him to his bedroom and plopped down on the rug in front of his bed. Tightening the belt of her robe, she got as comfortable as she could on the cold, hard floor. Even with the rug under her fanny, the old house was chilly. "Okay, what is it? If you're going to give me the song and dance that Dad really doesn't want to take this job, then don't bother. As far as I'm concerned, he'll do what he wants to do."

"But that's just it, C.C.," Eric said, flopping onto the bed. "He won't. He feels too guilty to do what he wants."

"How do you know?" she snapped. "Geez, since when do I have so much power in this family?"

"That's not the point," Eric shot back. "It's not about power, it's about him feeling like a failure because we had to sell our house and everyone had to go to work just to make ends meet."

"That wasn't my fault."

"It wasn't his fault, either," Eric exclaimed. "For crying out loud, Dad's not responsible for losing his job. He worked his butt off for TechniQuik for years! But did they care or appreciate it? Hell no. The minute they could find a way to cut costs and increase profits, they dumped him and a whole bunch of others, not caring that they were ruining lives."

"What's that got to do with this new job offer?" Courtney asked.

"Because it's likely the same thing will happen," Eric said. "At least with the video store he's doing something he really likes, he's enjoying himself. For a man like Dad, there are always going to be plenty of video store jobs; he knows more about movies than anyone this side of the UCLA film school."

Courtney looked down at the rug. Much as she hated to admit it, even to herself, Eric was right. Her father did like working in the video store. He liked writing his column for the newspaper and being asked to speak at the library. He liked having time to enjoy life. Heck, he'd even told Courtney he was thinking about taking one of those extension courses in film at UCSB.

"I'm not asking him to give up what he likes doing," she protested, fighting off another ugly wave of guilt. "He can still be Landsdale's resident movie expert."

"Not if he's working sixty to seventy hours a week he can't," Eric pointed out. "And what about the family? Do you remember what it was like before? Mom was an uptight housewife, Dad was working all the time, and you and I never even talked. We all led separate lives. Now we talk all the time. You and I do projects together, Mom's doing something she loves and so is Dad. That's important, Courtney. Life is short. None of us knows what's going to happen next. For the first time in years, Dad's enjoying life."

"But he enjoyed earning a decent salary, too," she said. But even as she spoke the words, she realized she was grasping at straws. Her father was much happier now. They all were.

"Did he?" Eric shook his head. "Your opinion means a lot to him. He knows how Mom and I feel."

"So I'm the one that's going to be the bad guy here," she snapped, leaping to her feet. "Well, it's not going to work. I wasn't the only one who liked living in a beautiful house, I wasn't the only one who liked having nice clothes and money in my pocket and not having to take the damned bus. I'm not the only one who will benefit if Dad gets a good job." She whirled and stomped out of Eric's room.

But she couldn't sleep. Eric's and her mother's words kept coming back to haunt her. She tossed and turned and punched the pillow a couple dozen times before completely giving up.

She tossed back the covers and climbed out of bed. She might as well get a glass of milk. She went downstairs in the quiet house, taking care not to make any noise. Courtney opened the fridge and took out a carton of milk. She poured a glass and then sat down at the table. As she sat there in the silent kitchen, she kept thinking about the other times the whole family had been around the table. They'd swapped stories about all their weird and funny customers. They'd shared their hopes and dreams. They'd had fun together.

Courtney smiled in the darkness, remembering how just last week her mother had argued with an enthusiasm that bordered on passion that people with plants lived longer than people who didn't have them. That gardening was an act of creation just like writing a play or composing a song. They'd all kidded Eleanor and laughed and joked that night. But everyone had respected her point of view.

That memory led to another one, as memories often did, and Courtney found herself recalling how her father had talked about organizing a film club. Nothing grand, he'd said, but it would be nice if all the science fiction or 1940s film noir fans could get together once a month and talk about their favorite movies. She winced, wondering if he'd still have the time or the energy to do something like that if he was commuting to Thousand Oaks every day. Courtney didn't know what to think anymore. She got to her feet, rinsed her glass out, and went back upstairs.

But even the milk didn't help her sleep. When she

finally dozed off, it was almost time to get up. The next morning her head hurt and she was tired. Not wanting to face either her mother or her brother, she dressed quickly and went for a walk.

But she couldn't get away from her conscience. She kept thinking about her father, about how he laughed so much now and how she'd spotted him sitting at his desk in the family room, happily scribbling away on that film article for the local paper.

Courtney didn't know what to do. She came home and spent the rest of the morning cleaning the bathroom. By the time she walked into the Victorian Café later that day, her nerves were so wound up she was amazed she could carry a cup of coffee without spilling it. But she did. Despite being tired and uncertain, she was able to do her job.

"Hi, Courtney," David said cheerfully as he walked in, a jacket slung over his arm. "You like Mexican food?"

"I love it," she replied.

"Good, there's a great restaurant over near the college. We can try it Saturday night if you like."

"That would be great," she said, smiling brightly.

Whistling, he disappeared into the back.

Courtney turned to get the coffeepot. As she reached for it, she happened to catch Henry's eye. The cook was smirking at her, his grizzled face plastered with a wide, silly grin.

"What are you so happy about?" she asked suspiciously.

"Young love," he sighed dramatically and rolled his eyes. "Ain't it grand. It does my old heart good to see you young people courtin'."

"Oh, can it, Henry," Courtney said, smiling in spite of her turmoil. "It's only a date."

"Yeah, but it's been a long time comin'."

She wondered what he meant but didn't want to ask him. The last thing she needed to top off a pretty crummy day was for David to come out and catch her pumping the cook about him.

"What's been a long time coming?" Mavis asked.

Courtney whirled around. She hadn't even heard the front door open. "Hi, Mavis," she said brightly, trying to head off Henry before he told the whole world about her and David's date.

"Hi, dear." Mavis took her usual spot at the counter and then looked at the cook. "Answer my question, Henry."

"Courtney and David's big date," Henry replied in a voice loud enough to wake the dead.

"Oh that," Mavis waved her hand dismissively. "I already knew about it."

"How?" Courtney asked.

"David told me," Mavis grinned.

Courtney gaped at her. Did the whole darned restaurant know about their date?

Mavis, seeing Courtney's face, laughed. "Don't look so surprised, dear. We've all known David's had a crush on you since the day he hired you."

"He hid it well," Courtney replied dryly as she reached for a coffee cup for Mavis. She poured the coffee, cut a thick slice of cake, and put it on the counter in front of the elderly woman. "The way he acted when I first got here, you'd have thought I had the bubonic plague."

"Thank you, dear," Mavis said and picked up her fork. "Of course he did. He couldn't let his feelings show, could he? David's a gentleman."

"He could have been a bit friendlier."

"Nonsense. He was the perfect employer," Mavis

said stoutly. "You must understand, David couldn't let you know he liked you and wanted to ask you out. He has integrity, you know. You were his employee."

"I'm still his employee," Courtney countered.

"But your date's not until Saturday night and by then, he won't be your boss anymore," Mavis grinned triumphantly. "He's a rare one, my dear."

"Yeah." Courtney smiled broadly. "He's pretty cool."

"You do have a way with words, my dear," she said laughing. "But he's a bit more than that. Why, if I were sixty years younger and single I'd give you a good run for your money for that young man's attention. He's that rarest of creatures. He's handsome, hardworking, honorable, and filled with integrity. You could do much worse in this old world."

"For goodness' sake, Mavis," Courtney exclaimed. "It's only a date."

Mavis delicately took a bite of angel food cake. "But one date can lead to another and another. He's quite smitten with you, you know. Not just because you're pretty, either."

"Oh, he likes my mind, does he?" Courtney asked. What the heck. So what if he came out and heard them talking about him? He wasn't going to fire her.

"Possibly," Mavis replied. "But what I meant was, David quite admires your character."

CHAPTER
TEN

December 23rd

Dear Diary,

Mavis really blew me away today. David admires my character! I'm not sure whether that's good or bad. Would he still admire me so much if he knew how self-centered I can be? Am I being selfish? Is it so bad to want a nice life? Darn. Why is everything so hard? Why can't things come in nice, neat little packages without all these complications? A couple of months ago, everything was so simple. I wanted my old life back. Now I'm not so sure. If Dad had never lost his job, I'd have never worked at the Victorian Café. I'd never have met David or Mavis or Henry. I keep thinking about everything the way it is now. Eric and Mom are right, we are much happier than we used to be. But couldn't we be just as happy with Dad earning more money?

Courtney stared at the words she'd just written and knew the answer. She closed her diary, tossed it aside, and lay listening to the silence of the quiet house. Eric and her mom were already in bed and Dad was working a late shift.

Courtney tossed her covers aside, climbed out of bed, and put on her robe. Moving softly, she went downstairs and into the kitchen. Picking up the tea kettle, she filled it with water and put it on the stove to boil.

A few minutes later, she heard the front door open and close. Her father's footsteps came down the hall.

"Hi, honey," he said. Surprised, he stopped in the kitchen doorway. "What are you doing up so late?"

"There's no school, remember? It's Christmas break, so I can sleep in tomorrow morning. I thought we could have a cup of cocoa together."

"Good idea," he said, dumping his lunch box on the counter as he walked to the table. "I could use something hot tonight. It's cold out there. Hard to believe Christmas will be here soon, isn't it?"

"Yeah, just a couple more days. I'm glad Eric put the lights up out front last week."

"I helped," Jack protested. "I held the ladder."

"And you carried the tree in too," she added, laughing.

"That was one heavy tree." Jack yawned. "I don't know why your mother had to have a live one this year. The pot alone must have weighed twenty pounds."

"Come now, Dad, you didn't think Our Lady of the Plants would let a dead one in this house, did you?"

The kettle boiled and Courtney took it off the stove. She pulled a box of instant cocoa out of the cupboard, emptied a packet in each mug, and then poured the boiling water over it.

Jack sat down and stretched, groaning as he kicked off his shoes. "My feet hurt. I didn't get a chance to sit down all evening."

"Yeah, we were pretty busy too," Courtney said. She yanked a spoon out of the top drawer and stirred the cocoa. "I need to talk to you, Dad," she said as she carried the steaming mugs to the table.

"I know, honey." He smiled gently. "But before you say anything, I want you to know I understand why you want me to take this job offer."

"You do?"

"Absolutely. I've decided you're right," he said. "I'm calling them tomorrow and accepting."

"Don't do it," she said quickly.

He looked at her curiously. "But I thought you wanted me to."

"I did. I mean, I did at first," she sputtered, trying to get the words out fast before she changed her mind. "Before I had time to think about what it would do to all of us."

He peered at her closely, his eyes searching her face. "Have Eric and your mother been badgering you?"

"No," Courtney protested, then she shrugged when she saw the look of disbelief spreading across his face. "Okay, maybe a little. But it wasn't really badgering. It was more like they pointed out some of the disadvantages of you going back to corporate work. Don't be mad at them, Dad. They were thinking of you."

"I know they meant well," Jack agreed with sigh, "but they really shouldn't have said anything. This is my decision."

"But if affects all of us."

"I'm aware of that, honey. But it affects me the

most. Look, there's something else you better understand." Jack leaned forward. "My taking this job
isn't just about the family and what it would mean
to our financial situation. It's about me."

Surprised, she stared at him. "Do you want the
job?"

"Part of me does," he said bluntly. "I'm forty-eight
years old and I'm a clerk in a video store. That's not
exactly how I'd planned on spending my life."

"But I thought you liked your job," she protested.

"I do. But there's another part of me that liked
being a hotshot executive. That liked wearing a suit
and tie and having a secretary. . . ." He trailed off
and looked away, gazing out the window into the
black night. "But there was a part of me that hated
it too. Hated the boring meetings, the long hours,
the petty office politics, and the constant jockeying
for position." He laughed cynically. "Stupid, isn't it.
A man my age and I don't know what to do when I
grow up."

She didn't know what to say. All along, she'd
thought it was because of her that he was considering the offer. But now she realized she'd been
wrong. "You are a grown-up," she said quietly. "You
always have been. You've taken care of all of us, no
matter what happened, and you did a good job too.
We all turned out pretty nice."

"Thanks, honey. That's good to know."

"When do you have to make a decision?"

"By tomorrow." He yawned and rubbed his hand
over his chin. "The fact is, that job pays three times
what I'm making now. That money would sure come
in handy, too."

"We've done okay without it," she replied.

"Come on, Courtney, be honest. I know you've

hated the fact that we're a lot poorer these days. We've survived. But you've had to give up an awful lot of things."

"Like what?" she challenged. "A class ring. Senior pictures. A dress for the Winter Ball. Get real, Dad, those are pretty petty things when you compare them to what I've gained."

Jack stared at her a moment, his expression thoughtful. "What do you feel you have gained?"

This was the tough part. How to explain it without sounding like some ditzy goody-two-shoes? Courtney wrapped her hands around her cocoa mug and picked it up. "For starters, Eric and I are a lot closer these days. It used to be we hardly even spoke," she said, smiling softly. "Now we're riding the bus together, talking all the time, and even redecorating the house without killing each other."

"You've both grown up a lot," Jack said with a laugh. "And even if I took this job, you could still be close."

"But that's not all," Courtney persisted. She had to make him understand. "What about Mom? She loves her job. Getting out of the house has turned her into a totally different person. She doesn't even nag anymore . . . well, not as much as she used to, anyway."

He tossed a quick glance over his shoulder toward the kitchen door and then grinned. "Okay, you're right about that too. But she could still keep her job. I think that's what's made her happy."

"That's not the only thing that's made her happy," Courtney pointed out. "You have. Your being home and spending time with her. God, you two have been acting like a couple of lovebirds—you run around holding hands and even kissing."

"I'd still spend time with her," he countered quickly. "Maybe not as much, but enough. Believe me, I know my relationship with your mother has improved. I wouldn't do anything to jeopardize that."

She racked her brain for another argument. She couldn't believe she was sitting here, trying to talk him into turning down a hotshot management job, but she was. "All right," she said, "what about you?"

"What about me?"

"Do you want to spend two hours a day in the car, stuffed into a suit and tie, to go do something you don't like?"

"I didn't hate my old job," he replied.

"Yeah, but you didn't love it, did you?" She put her mug down. "You love films, Dad. I know that running a video store isn't like being a movie director or anything, but it's a foot in the door. Where is it written in stone that you have to spend the rest of your life behind a video counter? Why couldn't you take some night classes in film and keep on writing columns for the local paper and see what happens?" The words poured out in a rush. "Nobody knows what the future holds. At least now you're doing something you genuinely like. There's always the chance it could lead to something else. As my friend Mavis always says, life's short and none of us know how many heartbeats we've got left."

"That's a cheery thought."

"But it's true," Courtney shot back. "Why spend even one minute of your life doing something you don't love if you don't have to?"

Jack leaned forward on his elbows. "There are other considerations, you know. College for one. If I take this job, you could probably go to Prior and

Eric could apply to Harvard. I can hardly send you away to school on a video store clerk's salary."

"Video store manager," Courtney corrected. "You were offered a promotion, remember? Besides, we can get decent educations right here."

He raised an eyebrow. "Landsdale JC isn't Prior or Harvard."

"But it's a good school," she said defensively. "And Eric really doesn't give a hoot about Harvard; he told me so."

"When?" Jack asked suspiciously.

"A few weeks back," Courtney replied truthfully. "We were talking about the fact that I was going to have to go to Landsdale and that it didn't bother me anymore. Eric said he'd decided to go there too. That there was no point in going off somewhere to college when he could live at home for the first two years and save his cash."

Jack shook his head. "Honey, I know what you're trying to do and I appreciate it, but this is going to have to be my decision."

Courtney got up. There was no more she could say. She'd given it her best shot. "I know," she said softly. "But I thought it was important to let you know how I feel. I don't want you to take this job. You'll hate it."

Courtney was on pins and needles all day. Her father had gone off to work without telling anyone what his decision would be. She hung around the house until the last minute, hoping he'd call home so she could ask him what he'd decided, but the phone didn't ring once. She gave it one last chance as she was heading for the front door—she hovered in the hall a minute or two before taking off for the bus stop at a run.

Distracted and worried about her dad, she barely noticed that David seemed to be finding a lot of excuses to be out on the floor with her. He brought the time cards out to the counter instead of doing them in the office. When that little chore was done, he hung around, shooting the breeze with the regulars and drinking coffee. He even helped during the dinner rush.

Finally it was time to clock out. Courtney flew down the hall, snatched her time card off the rack, and shoved it in. She grabbed her backpack out of the locker, slammed the door shut, and started to charge toward the front door. She ran smack into David.

Laughing, he grabbed her shoulders. "Hey, what's the rush?"

"I have to get home," she said, giving him a quick smile. "I don't want to miss the bus."

"Don't worry about it." He released her and stepped toward the office. "I was going to offer you and Eric a ride. Hang on a minute and I'll lock up the office."

"Okay." She waited impatiently while he turned off the office lights and locked up.

They met Eric as they came out the front door. "David's giving us a lift home," she told her brother.

"Cool," Eric mumbled, even as he gave her a sour look.

David walked on ahead of them, getting his keys out to unlock the door for his passengers. The moment he was a few feet away, Courtney leaned toward Eric and said, "I talked to Dad last night and

I told him I didn't want him to take the damned job."

Eric shot her a quick, surprised look. "No kidding?"

"Would I kid about something like that?" She broke off as they reached David's Toyota.

"You guys in a hurry to get home?" he asked as she and Eric climbed into the car.

"Yeah," Eric said quickly, shooting another fast glance at his sister. "We've kinda got to get home tonight. Christmas stuff and all that, you know."

"Sure." David got behind the wheel and put the key in the ignition. "I should get home too. My mom wants me to help her wrap some presents."

They talked about Christmas and what shifts everyone had to work on Christmas Eve on the short drive to the Cutlers' house. David pulled up in front.

"Thanks for the ride," Courtney said as she got out. She pushed the front seat up so Eric could get his long legs out of the backseat without tying himself into knots.

"Hang on a minute, will you?" David said to her.

"Guess that means you want me to go inside, huh?" Eric said, grinning wickedly.

"Well, duh, Eric," Courtney said, making a face at him. But he only laughed, waved a goodbye to David, and ran for the front porch. She stuck her head back into the car and smiled expectantly.

David just grinned at her.

"Well," she demanded, "you asked me to hang on. . . ."

He leaned over and gave her a quick kiss. "I just wanted to say good night."

Stunned by the unexpected kiss, Courtney mumbled, "Uh, yeah, good night." She stumbled a little as she walked toward the house. David didn't pull away from the curb until she was safely inside.

Courtney ran for the kitchen.

They were all there, seated in their usual spots around the table.

"We've been waiting for you," her father said, his expression serious.

Her heart sank. She didn't like the look on his face. She didn't like the look on any of their faces. Quickly she dashed to her chair and plopped down. "Okay, I'm here."

Jack took a deep breath. "I know all of you have been waiting to see what I've decided to do about this offer. But please keep in mind that, whatever my decision, I really appreciate everything—"

"Jack," Eleanor interrupted impatiently. "Cut to the chase. We've been on pins and needles all day. Just tell us, please. You can give us as many speeches as you like afterwards, but for God's sake, put us out of our misery."

"Yeah," Eric chimed in. "This waiting's killing me."

"Oh rats, I had the best speech prepared too. But if you insist." Jack laughed. "Okay. I told Tarleton I didn't want the job. You are now looking at the manager of Wildheart Video Store."

They had the best Christmas of their lives that year. Courtney didn't know whether it was because everyone was relaxed or just sheer relief that they'd survived. She really didn't care.

About a week after David's final day at the Victorian Café, Courtney stood behind the counter, filling salt and pepper shakers.

"I bet you really miss David, don't you?" Mavis asked.

Courtney shrugged. "Not really."

Mavis's eyes widened in surprise. "How extraordinary. You mean you don't miss him at all?"

Courtney screwed the lid back on a pepper shaker and then carefully dusted her hands on the towel she had tucked in the waist of her apron. "No. Why should I? The new boss is really nice. I like him a lot."

"He seems a nice enough man." Mavis's brows drew together in a puzzled frown. "But I was sure there was something growing between you and David. I was certain of it."

Courtney couldn't stand it anymore. She burst out laughing.

"Aha," Mavis exclaimed with a triumphant grin. "Try and tease the old lady, will you?"

"I'm sorry, I couldn't resist."

"You're forgiven," Mavis said. "But only if you tell me all about it."

"There's not much to tell—we've been dating, that's all," Courtney replied. Mavis was almost as bad a gossip as Henry. If Courtney told her everything, the whole restaurant would know before the woman finished her second cup of coffee.

"Are you serious about one another?" Mavis asked bluntly.

Courtney picked up the tray of shakers and turned to put them on the back counter. Glancing up, she saw Henry watching them. He was unashamedly eavesdropping. "For goodness' sake, we've only gone out twice." But it was more than that, and both she and David knew it. They had something special. They called each other every day. She knew deep in her bones that her relationship with David was more serious than any she'd ever had before.

"Is he going to ask you to the Winter Ball?" Mavis asked. "Can I have another cup of coffee, dear."

Courtney grabbed the pot and refilled everyone at the counter.

"Well," Mavis demanded, when Courtney got to her, "is he?"

"He already has," she admitted with a huge grin.

"Wonderful."

"But I'm not sure I'm going to go."

Mavis's mouth dropped open. "Not go? But that's absurd. You've talked about wanting to go for months."

"That was before I saw the price of evening gowns," Courtney said honestly.

"Goodness, child," Mavis said, shaking her head. "You mustn't let something like that stop you from having an evening with your young man. An evening, I might point out, that'll you'll remember for the rest of your life."

Courtney sighed. She'd given it a lot of thought ever since David had asked her. The truth was, she had plenty of money in her savings account and she could probably make enough in tips in the next two weeks to buy a nice dress. But she wasn't sure she wanted to anymore. "I know I'd remember it forever. But let's face it, I work hard for my money. I'm just not sure laying out the kind of cash a new dress would cost is worth it. Don't get me wrong, Mavis. A few weeks ago I'd have jumped at the chance to go, and damn the expense. . . ." She paused, not sure of what she was trying to say.

"And now you're not sure that even a precious memory is worth what it would cost you?" Mavis finished. "Yes, I quite understand. Those of us on limited budgets do have to pick and choose a bit carefully in life, don't we."

"That's it, that's it exactly. I didn't use to have to pick and choose, I mean, I used to always have money for stuff," Courtney said seriously. "Now that I do, I guess I'm just a little more careful."

Mavis picked up her coffee and took a sip. Her face was puckered in concentration. She put the cup down and smiled up at Courtney. "What time do you get off?"

"Seven. Why?"

"Good, then I'll expect you at my house at seven fifteen."

"Your house? But why?"

Mavis smiled broadly. "Because, my dear, I'm going to be your fairy godmother."

"Oh my God, Mavis, I can't wear this." Courtney held her breath as she looked at her reflection in the full-length mirror. "What if I ruin it?"

"Are you in the habit of ruining clothes?" Mavis asked.

"Well, no," Courtney said. "But I've never worn a dress like this either. God, I'll be scared to move."

"Don't be, it's quite sturdy. I've reinforced the original material with new cloth and these beads are hand sewn, my dear. Nothing short of a good pair of pinking shears will get them off." She tucked another pin in the hem. "That ought to do it. I'll do up this hem for you and you can pick the dress up tomorrow. How will that be?"

Courtney couldn't believe it. "Are you sure? I mean, this dress must be worth a fortune."

"Only to a collector, dear." Mavis slowly climbed

to her feet. "It was worn in the film *Laura* but not by any of the major stars." She stepped back and surveyed her handiwork. "You look quite lovely, my dear. But it is an old-fashioned dress. I'll understand if you don't want to wear it."

"Oh no," Courtney yelped. "I want to wear it. I'm just scared I'll mess it up." She turned back to the mirror. The dress was a delicious light blue satin overlaid with hundreds of hand-sewn beads and sequins. Floor-length and slinky, it hugged her slim figure like a second skin. When she walked into the Winter Ball, she'd knock their eyes out. If for no other reason than that she'd be the only one in the room wearing a fifty-year-old gown. It would take nerve to wear a gown this different to the ball, but Courtney didn't care. She loved it. More important, she was so touched by the gesture that rather than hurt Mavis's feelings, she'd have worn the dress even if it looked like last year's rag bag. So what if she didn't get crowned queen of the ball, this dress was so spectacular that wearing it would be an honor.

"What kind of shoes should I wear with it?" As she wasn't having to pay for a new gown, it wouldn't hurt her to spring for a new pair of shoes.

"High-heeled silver sandals," Mavis said firmly. "And drop a few hints to David about the color of the gown—we wouldn't want him showing up with an inappropriately colored corsage."

"Hey, Courtney, David's here. He's wearing a monkey suit," Eric yelled.

Courtney took a deep breath, picked up the small, silver beaded bag that went with her new shoes, and gave herself one last look in the mirror. It was now or never. Slowly she opened the door and stepped into the hall. No one, not even Allison, had seen her dress. She hoped she wasn't getting ready to make a fool of herself in front of all her friends.

She took another calming breath as she got to the head of the stairs. David, along with the rest of her family, was standing at the bottom.

David's eyes widened.

Eric's jaw dropped.

Her mother was smiling and her dad had a grin wide enough to split bricks on his face.

"Well," she said hesitantly. "How do I look?" She'd done her hair in soft curls around her face and she was wearing an old-fashioned, fifty-year-old dress and a pair of silver sandals. She probably looked ridiculous and none of them knew how to tell her.

"Wow." Eric broke the stunned silence. "That dress is even cooler than the one in the rental store window. You look great, C.C. Like something out of an old movie."

Courtney smiled and started down the stairs.

"You look wonderful, honey," her mother said. "And I love your hair that way."

"You look like something out of an elegant, nineteen forties movie," her father said. "Like Gene Tierney or Gail Russell. . . ."

"This dress is from a nineteen forties movie," she said. "Mavis lent it to me. She's had it wrapped in plastic for the last fifty years." She reached the bottom of the steps and faced David.

He still hadn't said anything. She couldn't tell whether he was struck dumb because he'd be taking a freak to the ball or because he was awestruck by her beauty.

"You're absolutely beautiful," he murmured finally. His eyes met hers and she saw that he wasn't being polite. He really meant what he'd just said.

"So you're not embarrassed to be taking a girl wearing a fifty-year-old dress to the ball?" she said lightly.

He laughed. "I'd want to take you to the ball even if you were wearing a hundred-year-old dress."

"Gag me with a spoon." Eric made choking noises. "God, David, you don't have to lay it on with a trowel. She looks cool, but she's just Courtney."

"That's enough for me," he said softly.

The ball was held in a fancy hotel in Santa Barbara. David helped her off with her coat and she took his arm.

"You ready?" he said.

"Yep, I think we make a pretty darned handsome couple. You look yummy in a tux. You should always wear one."

"Yeah, right. This will probably be the last time you ever get me in one of these things." He led her from the coatroom toward the double doors leading to the ballroom. As they walked through the crowd gathered in the foyer, Courtney could see heads turning. Her gown did stand out a little.

"I don't think our chances of getting voted queen and king are very good," she whispered. Hillary Steadman was gaping at her from across the foyer. Courtney saw her poke Maxine Frankel in the ribs and point in their direction. She gave Hillary a wide smile and a wave.

"Do you care?" David asked.

"No," Courtney shot back. "I would have four months ago, but now, just being here with you is enough." And that was the real truth. Just being there was enough. She didn't have to be the best, she didn't have to have the best, she only had to be herself.

As soon as they got into the ballroom, David pulled her out onto the dance floor. They danced slow, locked close together and moving in time to the music.

It was magical. It was wonderful and she never wanted it to end. Heads turned as David whirled her around the floor. People openly gaped at her dress, some of them with smiles on their faces and some of them looking puzzled as to why she'd choose to wear such a strange outfit to the Winter Ball.

But Courtney felt like a queen. The music stopped and she and David headed for the punch bowl.

"Courtney, that dress is fabulous," Allison gushed as she and Jared came up behind them. "Everyone's talking about it. Where did you get it?"

"A friend lent it to me," Courtney said proudly. "It's over fifty years old."

She introduced Allison and her date to David. The four of them made a night of it. Courtney was amazed at the number of people who loved her dress. After a while, she felt a bit like Cinderella. "I'm almost afraid of midnight," she whispered in David's ear as yet another classmate asked her where she'd gotten her gown.

"Why? You think you'll turn into a pumpkin?"

"No, I'm afraid this dress will disintegrate into rags and I'll end up wearing nothing but my underwear."

"I wouldn't mind that." He laughed and twirled her toward the doors leading out to a terrace.

"Though I would like a little more privacy for the event. Come on, let's go outside for some fresh air."

"I really don't think the dress is going to shred, David," she said as soon as they got outside. "Honestly."

"Hey," he said as he gave her a cocky grin, "you can't blame a guy for hoping. Are you having a good time?"

"Wonderful."

"You didn't mind us not being voted king and queen?"

"Nah," Courtney said honestly. "Leave that to Hillary and her date. God knows she worked hard enough for it."

"I'm glad you're enjoying yourself," David said. "I am, too." He put his arm around her and they walked to the edge of the terrace. "I hope it's the first of a lot of good times for us."

"I do, too, David." Courtney sighed. "But you never know, do you? Tonight we're together and that's what's important. Nobody knows what the future holds."

He gave her a quick, puzzled look. "What does that mean?"

She laughed at his expression. "Oh, David, all it means is that if I've learned one thing, it's that there's no guarantees in life. Who knows what tomorrow will bring? I hope we're together for a long time—"

"I do, too," he interrupted. "I really like you."

"And I like you," she responded. "But both of us know how unpredictable life can be. Five months ago I was a totally different person than I am now. Five months from now I might be someone completely different."

"I hope not," he said, tugging her closer. "I like this Courtney. But I know what you mean. There aren't any guarantees. Not for any of us."

"I can guarantee you one thing," she said, turning and brushing a kiss lightly on his chin. "I'll remember tonight for the rest of my life." She would, too. No matter what happened between her and David. No matter what curves life tossed her way. Tonight was one of those sweet, precious memories that would be with her forever. Courtney knew something else about life too. Something she didn't share with David because she sensed he knew it too. Life wasn't about things, it was about people.

"Me too. Maybe if we're lucky," he said softly, "fifty years from now we'll be remembering it together."

If you enjoyed

No Guarantees

by Cheryl Lanham

Don't miss

JANINE AND ALEX, ALEX AND JANINE

by Michael Levin

*Here is a special excerpt from the exciting novel
coming in October from Berkley Books*

Monday, September 1

My social life to date:

We went to a party? My friends and me. My friends and I. Whatever. My so-called friends, from the high school that, thank you God, I no longer have to go to. Because we moved this summer. Not far, just a few towns over so my father can have a shorter commute. What a break for me that he got promoted and we had to move. You'd think I'd be nervous, starting my senior year of high school in two days at a brand-new school where I don't know anybody, and where people don't know what happened.

Or what didn't happen.

If anyone does know about it at the new school, I'll die. I'm not kidding.

Well, okay, it's not that big a deal. I won't die. I shouldn't blow it up into something earthshaking. It was just me getting totally and permanently humiliated, and then practically everyone in the school knowing about it. I mean, even freshmen were coming up to me the Monday after it happened and bagging on me. And my so-called friends thought it was the funniest thing they ever heard of.

That's why I'm so glad we moved, because I could see myself a hundred years from now at my tenth high school reunion and my so-called friends all going, "You remember the time when we were at that party at Dave's house?" and I'd just turn red and my kids would say, "Mommy, what happened? Why are they all laughing at you?" And then they'd find out and they'd laugh at me, too. I'm not exaggerating. I swear.

So we're at this party and all my so-called friends know I have this massive crush on this one particular boy. His name is Eric, if you must know. Have I ever said anything to him? Are you kidding me? Are you insane? No, I never said anything to him. Is he cute? Yes, very.

He has gorgeous brown eyes and wavy brown hair and a really cute butt, and he dresses like a model in a fashion magazine. It always amazes me when boys have any sense of style, because where do they learn it? Not from each other, that's for sure. Most of them, especially the boys my age, think that a football jersey and torn jeans are the height of style. But this one boy, Eric—he knows how to wear clothes. And he has this look in his eye that says he just knows about things, and that if you're incredibly lucky he'll show you what he knows.

He really does look like a fashion model, which is pretty amazing, because he's on the math team. I don't know why people think you have to be stupid to be good-looking, like you've got to choose between being smart and being attractive. I mean, who made that rule? I think it's really hot when a good-looking guy is smart. But that's just my opinion. Most of the girls I know like to be smarter than their boyfriends even if they don't try to get good grades or work hard in school. Being smarter than your boyfriend, I think, is just about being insecure. But I hear a lot of boys like going out with girls who aren't smart, for the same reason, so I guess we're all even.

So here's this boy Eric, who's smart and cute and funny—well, I don't know if he's funny, because I've never talked to him. Unless you count that one time at the party I'm trying to tell you about. You'd think I'd just get over it. But the trouble is that it really is my entire social life to date. So maybe he's funny and maybe he isn't, but he's smart and cute, and I guess he's popular with the other boys because whenever I see him in the halls he's always with a group of guys. Not that I'm paying attention to him every time he walks down the halls. Well, okay, maybe I am.

Well, past tense. Maybe I was.

This is what happened: I made the unbelievable mistake of just casually dropping into the conversation with those so-called friends that Eric seemed okay, for a boy. That's all I said. That he was okay. And instantly it was all over the school that I was totally in love with him and that I was basically sitting by the phone every day waiting for him to call, and that if he didn't call me eventually, I would go postal. And get a gun and wipe out the whole school.

Which wasn't true. I would never get a gun. But I have to admit I did spend a certain part of every day sitting by the phone.

Which is totally unlike me, because I don't like to talk on the phone, which makes me totally weird among my friends. My attitude is, I just saw you all day in school. I'd rather read a book. My friends say I read too much and that it's going to make me antisocial. I think hanging out with them is going to make me antisocial.

But I really did sit by the phone, with a book, so it wasn't like I was completely wasting my time, and I have to admit I was hoping he'd call.

I don't know where I ever got that idea. I guess everyone's entitled to one big mistake.

It's funny to me that boys think girls have all the power. But it's so not true. It doesn't even matter how good-looking or popular a girl is. It's totally up to the boy whether he's going to ask us out, or ask us out again, or kiss us, or whatever. It's so completely unfair. It's like you spend your whole life trying to look a certain way so that you'll be noticed, but not too noticed, if you know what I mean, because you don't want to be calling attention to the way you look, although you really do. Which makes me crazy. I mean, let's make up our minds, either we want attention or we don't.

I'll tell the truth even if no one else will. I want attention. I want people to notice the way I look. The only trouble is that I'm tall and kind of average looking and I'm probably too thin although I eat all the time—wouldn't you if your father managed a supermarket? I guess I metabolize well or something. I'm the only girl in the world probably who's not on a diet, which is something my friends hate me for. They're always dieting, which is insane because if they were any thinner, they wouldn't be there. They're all obsessed. They all want to look like models in fashion magazines.

Actually, I do, too, but I've never told them. Thank God. Because that would just be one more thing they'd make fun of me for. Even though they all want the same thing. To look like models.

So one of the girls hears that this guy Dave's parents are going out of town for the weekend and he's having a big party at his house, and it's like the whole grade is invited. And it's the second weekend of June, so classes are almost over, and if you want to have a boyfriend or a girlfriend this summer, this party is practically your last chance.

And then I hear Eric's going to be there.

I set a record. I got dressed, undressed, and redressed seventeen times. Okay, I exaggerate. Four or five times. I just wanted him to notice me.

I tried on this really short skirt that even my friends don't know I have. If I wore it, they'd just make fun of my legs. One time when I was a freshman, we were in the mall and I had this skirt on and this guy who was an adult actually looked at me and said, "Mm-hmm, your legs are too long." I know he meant it as a compliment, but excuse me: I was fourteen and I think it was the first time any guy ever noticed me that way. But for the next year all my friends called me "Too Long." They even bought a box of oolong tea, wrote the letter T in front of the word *oolong* so it spelled Toolong, and taped it on my locker.

I am so glad we're moving.

So all my friends are at this party, as is the whole eleventh grade practically. Everybody's spilling stuff and making a mess and the music is blaring and I figure when Dave's parents find out what happened, he'll be grounded for life. But no one cares, because it's a really good party.

By the way, I chickened out with the skirt. I ended up just wearing a pair of jeans and this yellow silk shirt I bought in a thrift store. I love buying funky clothing in thrift stores and then cutting them down and turning them into something. I actually found this clear plastic rain slicker for fifty cents in the same thrift store where I bought the silk shirt, which only cost a dollar. I cut the arms off the poncho and wore it over the silk shirt. It looked pretty good, I thought.

Of course, the other girls were like, "What are you wearing?" But I think they were just jealous because they didn't have anything imaginative on. They were wearing just normal stuff. Everybody in my high school is totally normal looking. I mean, they're nice clothes, but everybody's so afraid of looking the slightest bit different from everybody else. Except for me, of course. And of course except for Eric.

I saw him the minute I got to the party. The other boys were basically all wearing jeans and football shirts or shirts with basketball team names on them. Like half of those boys will ever be tall enough even to be a ball boy for a basketball team. But Eric outdid himself. He was wearing this totally prepped out white dinner jacket. I mean, a dinner jacket. With pressed jeans. He was the only boy with pressed jeans at the whole party. The boy was styling, and he's my age.

I didn't say anything to him about it—I sort of stayed away from where he was hanging out with his friends, because I didn't want it to look like I was coming on to him. I mean, it's totally unfair—if he comes up to me and starts talking to me, it's cool. But if I start talking to him, everybody's going to say I'm aggressive and I'm not feminine and I'm just wrong.

But I did get a look at the dinner jacket, and I noticed this barely noticeable stain on the back, and I realized I'd seen that dinner jacket before.

It was for sale in the thrift shop where I bought my outfit.

Eric shopped in the same thrift shop.

I know it sounds totally geeky, but I was like, this is meant to be. We'll be the best-dressed high school couple in America. We'll skip the malls with all the standardized clothing and just go to thrift shops and get really cool stuff and make amazing outfits for each other—I can sew—and we'll get into hot clubs and we'll have our pictures in magazines.

My friend Jody was like, "Are you even paying attention to anything I'm saying?"

No. I wasn't. I was just thinking about how much I had in common with Eric, and how could I conspire to be in a place where he could just say something to me, like, hey, how's it going, or nice outfit, or great party. I have to say that it felt demeaning to me that I couldn't just go up to him, that I had to work out this whole scenario in my mind of how I could position myself so that he could then decide whether he wanted to talk to me. I mean, who made up these rules in the first place?

Probably not boys. They'd probably be thrilled if girls came up to them and said stuff like, hey, how's it going, or nice Dallas Cowboys shirt, or, and I can't even imagine this, nice butt. It's probably tons of work being a boy because you always have to risk rejection. But at least they have the power to make things happen. We have to stand around. I bet girls made up those rules. Out of insecurity.

Well, whatever. Suddenly I had it all scoped out in my mind. The drinks and food and everything were in the kitchen. Eric and his buddies were hanging out by the fireplace, and my so-called friends and I were standing around by the front door. Like we had some place else to go, which we didn't. I would wait for Eric to go down the hall to the kitchen. Then I'd just time it so that by the moment he came out of the kitchen, I'd be going toward it. And the hall was pretty narrow, and people were hanging out in it, so we'd have to bump into each other.

He'd have to notice me.

And maybe he'd want to talk.

So Jody, who I met in fourth grade—she used to be really nice, but once we got into junior high she got really competitive. Not about grades, just about appearance. That's the funny thing about all my friends. We really were excellent friends all through growing up. It's only when we got to junior high that everything changed. We used to do all kinds of stuff—ice skating, tennis, even going to the library, and we would talk for hours about what we wanted to do when we grew up. But then everything changed, and suddenly the only thing that mattered to anybody was what everybody else looked like, or what they were wearing, or what boys were cute. Go figure that one out.

So that's why we were still together—because we used to be real friends. Now we were all like competitors in some kind of competition, except that none of us knew what we were competing for.

Well, at least, nobody told me. Anyway, Jody was telling this incredibly long story about I don't know what. Something that somebody said in this chat room. Chat rooms are incredibly lame except the ones where people talk about fashion, which I think is fascinating. There's one chat room dedicated to this teen model, Janine Adams—people say I look like her a little bit. Well, actually, nobody's said it, but I think it. If you must know, I had them start this particular chat room. I keep thinking, if I were Janine Adams, I wouldn't have to play stupid games to get attention from boys. But anyway, Jody stops in the middle of the story because she sees that every few moments I'm glancing—as discreetly as I can—right at Eric.

She looks at Eric and she looks at me. And then the other girls slide their eyes toward Eric, just taking these really subtle looks at him. And I'm dying because I'm afraid one of them is going to say something. Or worse, that one of them is going to go directly over to Eric and say, "Alex is staring at you. You know, Toolong. She wants you."

I give them all this really dark look, like, you better not say anything or I'll kill you.

That's when Eric went to the kitchen.

That's when I made my next mistake.

I told the other girls what I was going to do.

"I'm going to talk to him," I said quietly, trying to build up my courage. I told them because I thought they'd get behind me and encourage me.

Wrong.

"Eric's captain of the swim team," Carla said. She'd been my friend since first grade. "Why would he want to talk to you?"

I just glared at her. The other girls all cracked up.

I thought about not going over. But then the girls would just say I was chicken, and they'd make fun of me for that. I took a deep breath and made my way to the hallway.

"And you go, girl," I heard Jody say behind me.

"Mission impossible," Sheila said in this really smirking tone. I had been best friends with Sheila from fifth through seventh grades. We did all our science and social studies projects together for two years. Now all she did was stare at the way I dressed like I was some kind of moronic loser.

"Thanks for your support," I mumbled to myself, and I walked slowly into the hallway, trying to figure out the best place to position myself so that Eric would have to deal with me. What a moronic loser I was, I thought. I'm not even going to talk to him first. I have to find a place to stand so that maybe he'll want to talk to me. Who made these stupid rules? I thought. From now on, if I see a boy I want to talk to, I'm just talking to him.

Period.

I stood there in the hallway for almost forever. Eric must have been eating a seven-course meal in the kitchen. I glanced over at my friends, hoping for some moral support. Instead, they all just saw me looking at them and they all burst out laughing. Everybody else in the room stopped talking for a second and looked over at them. I nearly died—I thought they'd point at me. Fortunately, that level of cruelty was beyond them. But probably not by much.

Well, I waited and I waited and I thought, maybe Eric left the party by the back door and I'll be standing here all night, which will make me a total laughingstock. Or even just the fact that I've done this much—position myself to be noticed by a boy who wore stained clothing to a party—already I hated Eric, although I didn't really hate Eric, I just hated the rules. Fortunately, my so-called friends stopped laughing and went back to talking about whatever lame thing they were talking about, although every so often they would look back at me, like I was some sort of lab project they had to watch out of the corner of their eyes. I wanted to die.

And then Eric came out of the kitchen.

It was a pretty long hallway—it was a pretty big house. The whole scene happened like it was in slow motion. He stepped past this couple that was actually kissing in the hallway, which was pretty amazing to me because I don't think I'd ever seen a couple I knew kissing before in real life. They were just going at it. Eric sort of looked at them and just shook his head and laughed. I could hear him whisper to the guy, who was in my biology class, "Go get 'em, tiger."

Then all of a sudden he was about eight feet from me.

My mind was working like a million miles an hour. I realized if I didn't do something immediately, he'd walk right past me and I'd have wasted all my time and my friends would be in hysterics. And he'd probably even figure out from their laughing and pointing at me what I'd been trying to do.

I felt totally humiliated, and I hadn't even done anything yet.

But not as humiliated as I was about to feel.

So I just sort of casually eased into the middle of the hallway, like I was looking for something over his shoulder in the kitchen. I didn't move more than eight inches, and I knew I'd done it in a subtle enough fashion that he couldn't possibly have realized what I was up to.

I felt really proud of myself for being so smart and cool, and at the same time I felt completely less than human. I mean, all this, just so that maybe this guy would talk to me.

The music was still blaring and everybody was talking. Eric was now past the couple that was making out. He was getting closer and closer to me.

I, of course, was standing pretty much directly in his path, pretending to notice something in the kitchen.

He was two feet away.

He couldn't get past me. My plan was working perfectly. I knew without looking that my friends were watching us intently. I knew it.

And then he said something. To me. *Eric* said something to *me*.

I blushed beet-red. My knees went weak. I had never felt so dizzy and excited in all of my life. But the only problem was that the music was so loud that I couldn't hear what he said.

I know I had this goofy smile. "What?" I asked, grinning at him like I had some kind of fatal smiling disease. Where you can't stop smiling even if they tell you about dead babies or nuclear war.

He repeated himself. I thought he said "Dude" or "Groove," and I was trying to figure out what Dude or Groove in this context meant. It made no sense. You never call girls Dude, even if you're trying to be surfer-cool, which I supposed he was. And Groove? Who says Groove? What is he talking about?

I just kept that stupid smile on my face like out of sheer terror. I felt so stupid because I had to ask him again what he said. He was going to think I was a total idiot—and deaf besides. He'd never date me. Not in a million years.

"What did you say?" I asked, trying not to let the desperate way I felt leak into the way I sounded or looked.

He leaned forward and spoke directly into my ear. My heart was pounding so hard I thought I'd have a heart attack and die right on the hallway. He put his hand on my shoulder. Please keep in mind that I had never been even so much as touched by a guy before. And here was Eric, the coolest boy in creation, touching me, leaning over to whisper something incredibly cool and funny and romantic in my ear, and I knew that all of my so-called friends were watching and being jealous and eating their heart out.

I thought, God, take me right now. Let me die this second. Who cares if I'm still a virgin and never even kissed a boy. Eric is touching me, and he's about to ask me out on a date.

He leaned his mouth directly over my ear. I could feel his soft breath on my hair. I was exploding inside, fireworks, nuclear bombs, the Fourth of July.

He cleared his throat. I waited, breathless.

"I said, 'Move,'" he said, loud enough to blow out my eardrum. "You're blocking the hallway."

I just made this grunting sound, like, "ough ough." I couldn't believe it. No asking out. No funny romantic thing. No asking for my phone number.

He said move.

I thought, God, let me die right now.

Inside, my whole body just slumped over. If he'd hit me in the head with a can of soda at that moment, I wouldn't have noticed. And worst of all, I couldn't move. My feet—it's like Super Glue coated the bottom of my feet, and I couldn't move them a fraction.

Actually, I didn't want to move. I wanted to stand there and just punch his lights out. How dare he . . . toy with my feelings that way. Didn't he know how much I cared about him? Didn't he realize how much we had in common, how happy we could be, what great outfits we could wear? Didn't he realize we were meant to be together, the sun and the moon and the stars? Didn't he realize what I had to go through in my head and with my friends, just to be positioned so that he could sort of accidentally on purpose talk to me?

Didn't he realize how much *work* went into being a girl?

No, of course not. I wanted to kill him. But all he knew was that some tall, geeky girl in a weird outfit was blocking his path back to the living room. Boys don't know one one-hundredth of what we go through. They don't realize we give them all the power, every bit of it.

I wanted to throw up.

I just looked at him, hoping to convey with my eyes in a single look everything that I felt about him: desire, admiration, lust, infatuation, and intense interest, but also disappointment, regret, anger, misery, and suicide. He looked at me like, "What's up with you?"

Finally I stepped out of the way and let him pass. I didn't even move from the hallway. What was I supposed to do, go back to my friends and tell them what happened?

I just stood there, dreaming of joining the Peace Corps or the Foreign Legion and going to a small town a million miles away and helping the poor. Preferably in a country where there weren't any boys. At all. I would become devoted to the sick and the dying, and people would look at me and they'd know without asking that once upon a time a long time ago a boy had broken my heart.

Suddenly I remembered reading that Dr. Albert Schweitzer had set up a hospital in the middle of Africa somewhere, and volunteers came and worked there. That would be perfect—they all spoke French, so I wouldn't be able to understand them because I take Spanish. My life would be pure and chaste. I would wear black, so that people would think I was in mourning, like a Mediterranean widow. And boys would keep a respectful distance and never tell me to move.

I guess I was so deeply into my fantasy about Albert Schweitzer that I didn't notice that Jody, Carla, and the other girls had surrounded me.

"What did he say?"

"Did he kiss you?"

"Did he ask you out?"

"You're so brave!"

"What did he say?"

I looked at the floor, waiting for it to open up and swallow me whole.

"He said move," I said quietly, so quietly that none of them could hear me.

"He said what?" asked Carla.

"He said move," I said, and I could feel my face burning from shame. "I was in his way, and he told me to move."

There was this long pause-like moment as they all digested the incredible information I had just given them. And then all of a sudden they burst into the biggest laughter I had ever heard. They started laughing so hard that tears formed in their eyes. Everybody else in the party stopped talking to see what was so funny. Even the kids who were macking stopped kissing so they could see, too.

I wanted sincerely to die.

"He said move!" Carla exclaimed, sobbing with laughter.

"She was in the way!" Jody shrieked.

"I can't wait till I tell everybody!" Dani announced. Dani and I drew ponies and horses all the time in second grade. We were going to write a book together about horses and illustrate it ourselves.

"Psych!" said Carla.

"Busted!" Sheila laughed, wiping her eyes.

I couldn't take it anymore. I ran. Out of the hallway, out of the living room, out of Dave's house, all the way home.

And I cried for three straight hours. The phone never stopped ringing. I didn't pick it up, of course. I'd had enough.

I spent the whole weekend in my room and my parents nearly had to kill me to get me to go to school the following Monday. School was just the worst thing that day—I'm telling you, even freshmen who didn't know me came up to me and just pointed and said "Move!" The story must have gone around the entire school. Even teachers were smiling at me. My humiliation was complete.

I will never put myself in this position again, I thought grimly. I will never, I swear never, put myself in a situation where boys have total power. I don't care what the rules are, and I don't care if I never go on another date in my life.

Not that I've ever gone on one. Albert Schweitzer's hospital was looking better and better to me.

And all morning long, people just kept getting right in my face and saying Move! Move! Move!

I ditched my afternoon classes—who wouldn't, with everyone humiliating you like that. And just to show that there really is a God, that's the night my father came home from work to say that he'd been promoted, and that we were moving in time for the new school year. My parents were really concerned when they told me this, like, I'd be unhappy to leave my friends just before my senior year of high school.

Wrong. I was like, Mom and Dad, you're the coolest, let's pack up and go right now.

All those kids kept saying Move, Move, Move, and I just kept thinking, I'm going to Move. I'm going to Move out of this stupid town.

Well, we did Move, and we're in a house that's a little bigger than our last house, and school is just two days from now. I spent the summer working in my dad's supermarket as a checkout girl and I studiously avoided all contact with boys. I spent a lot of time in thrift shops, buying cool stuff and making great outfits. The only problem was I didn't have any friends and I didn't have anywhere to go. But I was definitely the coolest-looking checkout girl in the history of supermarkets. I spent a lot of time on the Internet, checking out the fashion sites, and I've downloaded a ton of photos of Janine Adams wearing really cool clothes. And I go in the fashion chat rooms almost every day, just to see what's up.

But every time I hear the word Move, I swear to God. I want to kill something.

I just pray—I just *pray* the kids in this school don't have any friends in my old school. If I hear the word *Move* one time, just one time, in the new school, I'm moving to Africa. Immediately.

I pray those kids don't know.

LIFE AT SIXTEEN

A dramatic new series

You're Not A Kid Anymore.

Life at sixteen isn't easy. That's why LIFE AT SIXTEEN tackles real issues you face every day. Family illness. Money problems. Broken homes. Whether you laugh or whether you cry, that's life.

___LIFE AT SIXTEEN:
BLUE MOON   by Susan Kirby
                                      0-425-15414-9/$4.50

___LIFE AT SIXTEEN:
SECOND BEST by Cheryl Lanham
                                      0-425-15545-5/$4.50

___LIFE AT SIXTEEN:
NO GUARANTEES by Cheryl Lanham
                                      0-425-15974-4/$4.50

VISIT THE PUTNAM BERKLEY BOOKSTORE CAFÉ ON THE INTERNET:
http://www.berkley.com

Payable in U.S. funds. No cash accepted. Postage & handling: $1.75 for one book, 75¢ for each additional. Maximum postage $5.50. Prices, postage and handling charges may change without notice. Visa, Amex, MasterCard call 1-800-788-6262, ext. 1, or fax 1-201-933-2316; refer to ad # 746

| Or, check above books and send this order form to:
The Berkley Publishing Group
P.O. Box 12289, Dept. B
Newark, NJ 07101-5289
Please allow 4-6 weeks for delivery.
Foreign and Canadian delivery 8-12 weeks. | Bill my: ☐ Visa ☐ MasterCard ☐ Amex _____ (expires)
Card#_____
Daytime Phone #_____ ($10 minimum)
Signature_____
Or enclosed is my: ☐ check ☐ money order |

Ship to:

Name_____
Address_____
City_____
State/ZIP_____

Book Total $_____
Applicable Sales Tax $_____
(NY, NJ, PA, CA, GST Can.)
Postage & Handling $_____
Total Amount Due $_____

Bill to: Name_____
Address_____City_____
State/ZIP_____